QUEEN OF DEMONS

BOOK FOUR OF THE CASTILLIAN BLOOD SERIES

KILLIAN WOLF

ISBN - 978-1-951140-07-6

Editor: Claerie Kavanaugh claeriekavanaugh.com/need-an-editor
Copyeditor: saltandsagebooks.com
Cover design: miblart.com
Formatter: Michael Davie

CONTENTS

FREE BOOK

Get the prequel free when you sign up for my mailing list at http://killianwolf.com/

As a reaper my life is simple . . .

Go where I'm told, help the dead move on. No bonding. No interfering with mortal affairs.

Collect, guide, rinse, repeat.

But when an escaped demon starts killing off a little boy's family one by one and affecting the balance of the universe, am I expected to stand by and watch?

Or should I save him, even at the expense of my existence?

WELCOME TO HAPS

ADDISON

*L*ocusts. Buzzing, swarming, biblical freaking locusts. But honestly, should I have expected anything else? Nothing even grows here, what does he think this'll do? Besides set off an alarm and let everyone know Lucifer is out of his cage. Oh, yeah, I guess that's the point.

Power surges through my arms, flames igniting my palms as an ocean of locusts swarms the yellow sky. In seconds, these giant flying monsters land on my skin, and my fire diminishes. Shit.

"Your power won't work against me, Addison. Go back to LLAPS and do what you're told."

I stumble back, raising my arms above my head and swatting furiously. The deafening buzz almost makes my ears bleed. I open my mouth to speak, to plea for him to stop. If nothing more.

"Lucif—" A locust flies into my mouth. I jolt back, spitting it out. I trip and tumble into the Akashic river.

The current pulls me under. Images of the past, present,

and future surface inside my mind's eye—yet I can watch it as if I were watching a movie. But not my past, mankind's.

In the beginning, there was no god, only particles of energy. Fast forward to humankind, and countless battles and wars over survival and territory. Lucifer stands alone on barren soil. He stands tall, semi-clad, with his chest covered in blood. He weeps over the blood loss of his brothers. He speaks, but I can't hear him. I don't have to. Here, I feel his emotions and know what is happening—almost like telepathy.

The image changes to a battleground. Dragons fly overhead, shooting fire. I duck my head. Holy shit . . . Those are definitely dragons! I spin around as metal clashes behind me and I yelp. Azazel, golden scythe in hand, swings it to a tall, ebony man wearing white and gold battle gear. Power sears through the man's arms and Azazel ducks it. Azazel's eyes move to mine and I wince. Can he see me? An arrow buzzes past me and my breath hitches as he catches it mid-flight before it hits his chest. A sigh of relief leaves my lungs. He can't see me; he was just looking past me.

He aims the scythe toward me, and a purple light zooms out of it. I turn around as a full-blown winged man crumbles to the ground. The other man yells as his friend turns to dust just like the Judge had when Azazel killed him.

A hoarse groan escapes the man's throat as he lunges toward Azazel, making him drop the scythe. Somewhere in the distance a fire blazes and a dragon roars. Azazel flicks his gaze in its direction, quickly kills the man, and makes a dash toward the dragon. I take a few steps to follow . . . curious to know what is happening. The fear in

Azazel's eyes when he heard that sound . . . Why are they fighting? A wave washes over me, and the scene becomes fuzzy . . .

Someone grabs my shoulders and pulls me up from the current. A soft pink glow seers in through the slits of my eyes. I blink a few times and a woman with a strong jawline and shoulder-length, curly blonde hair and green eyes comes into view . . . She looks familiar. But . . . it can't be . . . She looks like . . . my mom . . . I gasp and then start coughing. I struggle to sit up on my own and the woman helps me.

"Mom?" is all I manage to mutter.

A warm smile spreads on my mother's face and she nods. She has on gold and silver chest armor and holds a spear in her hand. "Are you okay?"

My knees quiver as I try to stand but I'm literally shaking. "But—I don't understand. How can you be here?" My mother had died of a heart attack when I was sixteen years old.

My eyes land on a half-opened white, stone temple in the distance. White stone slabs cover most of the ground except the flowing streams of the Akashic.

"You're in HAPS, *mija*. The current must have pushed you to the citadel when you fell into the water." HAPS . . . That's right . . . I fell when . . . Lucifer! Memories come flooding back and I shake my head. I'll deal with this later. Right now . . . I meet my mother's eyes.

My nose itches as I try to hold back my tears. "I can't believe this . . ." I wrap my arms around her neck. "I can't believe it's you."

My mom runs her fingers through my hair. "I've missed you so much. Come, follow me inside."

My legs automatically follow her. "Wait—what about Lucifer?"

"Yes, we're taking care of that now. We saw him coming from the Akashic waters. We knew you were here too. Come, follow me. I know you must have questions." Oh, so many questions!

Her body armor reflects off the pinkish-yellow glow of the sky. My brows squint: this is the same armor the men who were fighting against Azazel were wearing in my . . . vision? It sure as hell wasn't my memory. But I did fall into the Akashic, so it makes sense that it was a memory, just a . . . universal memory? Why is my mother wearing armor though? I follow her down a wide, white stone path, passing mountains to the left, to the white and gold marble temple.

Inside, my mom shows me to large white and gold cushions and throws on the ground.

"Where are we?"

"In my quarters."

"So, this is kind of like LLAPS?"

"Kind of, yes. Except this isn't a prison and not so damp and dark." My mother's smile radiates, and I smile back. This is unbelievable. I wish Dax were here . . .

She brings out a small cup of a hot beverage. "It's okay," she says. "You can drink this here. It's only jasmine tea."

I take the cup and the jasmine aroma fills my nostrils and my taste buds as I take a sip. I pause and look at my mom, whose eyes dance.

"Something happened when I fell into the river."

She nods.

"I saw . . ." I struggle for words. "Honestly, I saw so much I don't even know where to start."

"The Akashic holds the DNA of our universe. We use it to scry to look down on the people of Earth."

Huh. "In LLAPS they use it to scry as well, but for other reasons."

"I am aware."

"But there's something I don't get."

My mother nods and waits patiently; I take it as a cue to continue. There's such a calmness about her. Even at the mention of Lucifer being here, there isn't any hint of panic like there would be in LLAPS, or back home.

"In my vision . . . I saw the beginning of mankind . . . but I didn't see a god. Is there one? A god, I mean?"

My mother smiles. "We are god."

"I don't understand . . ."

"People are so consumed by what came before us. It doesn't matter. Humans created stories, and from those stories came power of belief. But magick, or energy, rather"—she waves her hands in the air—"is everywhere. Humans always knew how to call it down. Some just forgot. But we are the ones in charge up here. All of us."

My forehead creases. All of us. Before I get too wrapped up in what that means, my mind drifts to LLAPS. "So, the reapers . . . They weren't in that memory either." Except Azazel holding a scythe, but he didn't feel like a reaper there. But . . . Ambrose and Deacon said they were created to be in charge.

"The reapers were once all human. They just don't remember."

My breath hitches. Ambrose was a human? "They just forgot about it?" Woah . . .

She scrunches her brows. "That's how they wanted it."

Why wouldn't they want to remember? "So then why doesn't HAPS just tell them? Or remind them?"

"Because it's the way things have always been. They have a job to do and they serve their purpose."

My brows raise. "Wait, but Dax . . ."

A slanted frown falls on her face.

"Will he forget he was human too? Will he forget . . . about us?"

Her frown deepens. "Inevitably, yes. That's why I wanted him to come up here to be with me. But your father, bless him, called him back to Earth." She sighs. "And now he's a reaper—I did not want this for him."

My stomach churns . . . Dax is going to forget who he was, and become some robotic-acting reaper? That'll feel like losing him again. My throat closes. So much has happened though. I'm glad Ambrose had the Judge turn Dax into a reaper . . . I just didn't know it meant losing who he is. We thought maybe because he became a reaper after being dead, it would be different. But if the reapers were all human, it wouldn't be different for him . . . And now all this has happened . . . me becoming a demon . . .

I flick my eyes down to my cup. Does my mother know? How much has she seen?

"What's the matter?"

"Mom, I—"

"It's okay. I know everything, *mija*. It doesn't matter." She takes my hands and brings me back down to my seat. "You are still you."

". . . Still me." I quirk a brow. I have to ask. "Did you know about dad?"

"What do you mean?"

"About his demon blood? And how I have it too."

"Not while I was alive, but yes, I know all about the Castillian blood lineage. Demon blood runs deep in his side of the family."

Huh. No wonder the dagger got sent to us then. I guess Azazel's hopes at his escape from prison weren't far off. My mother offers me another calm smile and my eyes narrow.

I'm beginning to find it unsettling how my mother is acting like there isn't a care in the world. I mean, I want to feel the same calmness, but like . . . she knows I became a demon, and she's fine with it? She was never like this when she was alive. "What about Lucifer loose here in HAPS? You said you guys were taking care of it? Who else is taking care of it? And how?"

"We have an order put in place, like a safety for if and when this ever happened." The image of Azazel fighting men in armor . . . This armor flashes through my mind. The same armor my mother is wearing. They must have been angels . . . My mother catches me inspecting her clothes. So militant.

"What does that mean?"

"Trust me. We are far stronger than he is."

"But mom, what about me? He says I'm Queen of LLAPS. I don't want to be a demon queen. I just want to be me and go home."

My mom tilts her head to the side. "Whatever you choose to do, you have to be true to yourself. Addie, you are special." She reaches behind her and takes something out of a satchel. "I know LLAPS isn't the ideal place to be, but it doesn't have to be that way."

I screw up my face. Not the ideal place to be? Not . . . you need to go home and continue your nursing career? "What are you saying? That I should be Queen of LLAPS?"

"No, I'm just saying that you should follow your heart."

"Well, I thought I was, but it led me to the prison to find my boyfriend. And well . . ." I place my hand on my stomach and look down. My eyes fog up again. Should I tell her?

How much does she know? "Things turned out . . . differently." My throat clogs up.

My mother inches closer and throws one arm around my shoulder, bringing me in. I think she does know but doesn't want to say it. That's okay with me.

"Your life has changed, *mija*. But Addie, you must learn to forgive. I know what happened was horrible, and trust me, he will not go unpunished."

He? Does she mean Azazel? "But now you must make a choice and take charge of the new cards you've been dealt."

I take in her words. She's reminding me of Padrino. What choice do I have, though, really? If I don't save Earth, my home is ruined. Not just for me, but for everyone. But I won't rule LLAPS, I won't. "I just want everything to go back to the way it was."

"Well, maybe it can." She pulls away and shows me a small vial with a purple and gold liquid in it. "Accepting change and moving forward is the only option."

"What is that?"

"If you do not want to take up the mantle, Addie, then don't. We will take care of everything. I had one of our angel alchemists create a potion that will reverse your powers. You won't be a demon anymore and neither will your baby." She squeezes my shoulder and smiles.

My lips part as I clutch the potion in my hands. "I thought this couldn't be undone . . ."

"Anything is possible in HAPS. I figured you would want the choice, but if I were you . . . I would take it. Think of the baby."

I . . . have a choice. I stuff the vial in my pocket and wipe away a tear.

"What about Lorcan?"

"Who's that?"

"The reaper who—"

"Ah yes, we've been watching him too. We will send down our army."

I stifle a gasp. "So, you mean a war?"

"In a way. But they will stand no chance. Think of this as a quick cleanup. I'll have your brother brought up first."

My heart skips a beat. "Wait, can you . . . unreaper him?" Maybe this is a good idea. Fresh start. But what does she mean by a cleanup? What about Deacon and Ambrose? Would I be able to keep Skadi? "Mom, when you say a reset . . . What do you mean exactly?"

Screams shatter the walls and I flick my eyes to the open temple behind me. My mother gets up and runs out to the river. I set my cup down and follow suit. We approach the terrace facing the open plains and my jaw drops. Rivers of blood cover the Akashic waters of HAPS.

RIVER OF BLOOD

ADDISON

I stand frozen as the beautiful orange and yellow skies of HAPS turn dark red, reflecting the bloody waters that run through the Akashic rivers. I close my jaw and flick my eyes to my mother, who is already walking in the opposite direction.

"It's Lucifer," she says.

"Mom? Where are you going?" I rush to keep up.

"I need to close all the portals to HAPS. No one else gets in. No one gets out."

Uh, hold the phone. "No one gets out? You want to hold Lucifer here?"

"Yes, until we can seize him."

"Do you have a place that can hold him?"

She nods. "Yes, it's a holding facility until he gets moved back down to LLAPS." She marches over to a pillar and pushes her hand into the center. A hologram of a face appears in front of us. "Addison, you can't stay here. Before I do this, you should go straight home. I can open a portal directly there."

"But I just got here. I want to spend more time with you . . . Can't I stay and help?"

"I know, *mija* . . . but it isn't safe. And once I do this, all portals will be closed."

"Can't you just hold on a minute?" I yell.

She stops to look at me, her features hard, but her eyes caring. "Addison . . . there's no time."

"Who are you here? Why does this fall on you?"

"I help protect HAPS. So that others can enjoy their paradise."

I take a deep breath. "So, what's going to happen with Lucifer once you seize him?"

"We put him back in his dungeon. Where he can't hurt anybody."

"Won't he just find another way out? It's my fault he's out in the first place." I swallow hard.

"No, you can't blame yourself for that. He's a mastermind, Addie. And besides, his demonic son was the one who got in your head."

That's true. But still . . . I need to fix Earth and need Lucifer to do it. "You can't seize him yet. What about Earth? I came all the way here to get him to help me. There are literal demons and prisoners causing havoc back home. To fix that, I need him to fix LLAPS. And get everyone back where they belong," I stammer. *Did I just make it all the way to HAPS for nothing?*

The hologram floats in front of us, waiting for my mother to give a command.

"Initiate code red," she finally says.

"At once, Marina. You have 60 seconds to confirm."

I quirk a brow. Apparently, HAPS has a lot more tech than LLAPS does . . . Does LLAPS even have any tech? I suppose the scythes are techy . . . "What's code red?"

"While we seize Lucifer, our army will be going down to LLAPS to take care of the problem down there."

"What? Already?"

"Addison, we just spoke about this."

My heart pounds in my eardrums and suddenly I'm out of breath. "Wait!"

She stares at me, wide eyed and unflinching.

"Don't worry about your brother. He will be spared and brought up here."

Dread washes over me as all the souls I had tried to save cross my mind, all to be stolen back by Lorcan. Many of them didn't deserve it. Maybe they do deserve a chance at redemption. An image of Rezmelda emerges in my mind. I was cruel to her. But at the time, I believed it was warranted. Azazel must have really done a number on me because since becoming a demon myself, I now know demons aren't just evil creatures. They're a race, normally controlled. Maybe their deviant behavior has some merit to it. Maybe they too deserve a chance to live.

"What about all the souls down there?" I ask.

My mother's cheeks flush. "You mean the prisoners?"

"... Yes. What will happen to them?"

"We don't have time to weigh their innocence. We can't save them. This will be a fresh, clean start. Maybe some reapers will survive. They would have to go into the Akashic waters; the ones not tainted by blood." My mother holds her head. "Those rivers, ruined. HAPS is going to want to recuperate those waters and that will get messy."

"Get messy how?"

She purses her lips as she studies me. "Hm. Some things here are on a need-to-know basis, *mija*." What the hell does that mean? Need-to-know basis? Why can't she tell me?

"Can't the water just get filtered?"

She smiles and shakes her head. "Not this kind of water, unfortunately." I draw my brows together. The contaminated waters in the mental plane with the giant biting silverfish. Gross. Will that happen to HAPS?

"I know I don't have to ask if you care about what happens to the demons . . . but . . ."

"Oh, Addie . . . You were always so caring and nurturing. That's why you went into nursing." She places a hand on my cheeks, and I close my eyes. Even during all this torment, my mother has a way to calm my nerves. "But, killing them off will be what's best for the dimensions."

That brings me back to reality. "Eradicate them?"

"Not to mention that anything from LLAPS leaves behind a stench. Demons will get a whiff and come crawling out. We can't have that."

"A stench?" I sniff my shoulder. I don't smell anything.

"It's just a trail LLAPS leaves behind. It goes away the longer you've been away from there. Listen, once code red commences, that's what will happen. LLAPS will be levelled."

My bottom lip quivers as I stammer to speak.

"Addie, right now, Earth is getting worse. More human souls are dying, and demons are roaming free. This needs to stop now."

"Agreed. But what about the human souls that won't make it to HAPS?"

She shakes her head, leaving me to interpret her silence. She doesn't care. She really doesn't care. All demons, all prisoners, all potential demonic human souls will be turned to dust . . . or recycled, as Azazel put it to me once. I never thought I would find myself agreeing with Azazel, but he was right about one thing. Something needs to be done. But not in the way he wanted. "Call off the code red."

"What?"

"Call it off, please."

"I won't do that, Addison. This is the only way. It's what's best."

"I can't let you destroy LLAPS. There are reapers down there that I love!" I swallow as I push an image of Ambrose out of my mind. "And we can't just abandon all those souls."

My mom wrinkles her forehead. "Addison, if you take up that mantle, you can never live a normal life on Earth. You will have to stay in LLAPS, forever . . . I fear you won't be living the life you want if you do that. You won't be true to yourself. And that's all I want for you."

"I know. Which is why I'm not going to take up the mantle. But I still need to go down there, with your help."

She squints at me for a moment. "What do you have in mind?"

"Handle Lucifer. Let me handle Lorcan."

A sigh escapes her lips and her eyes dart from side to side. After a few moments, she speaks. "I can stall the code for twenty-four hours, but that's it. It's too much of a risk to let this go on for longer." She pauses. "How do you plan on stopping Lorcan on your own?"

I never needed Lucifer's help. He was right about that. Azazel helped me see it. "With my new powers, I can do anything."

My mother purses her lips. "You have twenty-four hours. If LLAPS isn't safe by then, I'm sending a team to collect you and your brother, and we're cleaning house. But hurry, I will be closing the portals."

"Is that twenty-four hours Earth time?" Every time I've left through a portal, time has moved a lot slower on Earth. I can use that to my advantage.

"Take this." My mother reaches behind the pillar and

pushes a hidden drawer open on the marble. She takes out a small hourglass and hands it to me. "Keep a close eye on this hourglass. When the last sand grain drops, you'll know it's too late."

I take the hourglass, giving her a tearful hug and then holding my hand out in front of me. Effortlessly, a portal opens, and I walk through.

A REAPING MYSTERY

AMBROSE

$\mathcal{M}$y gaze is fixed on the stone floor next to the podium of the High Reaper Courtroom, my grip tight around Deacon's scythe. Dax rests his hand on my shoulder, and I glance in his direction, smiling weakly. The council of reapers—or what's left of them for many have taken arms with Lorcan—murmur to themselves about what happened: Deacon's untimely and definite death.

"It wasn't your fault," Dax says. "No one could have been prepared for Lorcan using Deacon as a shield."

I straighten my spine. "I know, I just wish I could have done something. Pulled her out of the way, anything."

"I know how that feels. I am truly sorry."

And I know he is. I purse my lips and set Deacon's scythe down on the podium. "You're probably the only one who truly does understand, Dax. Look at them." I nudge my chin toward the reapers. "They don't mourn her. They can't. Empathy doesn't belong to reapers. Not usually."

"You're special for that, Ambrose. I know it hurts that she's gone, but don't start regretting the fact that you're different."

Different. Ever since a human I collected from the ice filled me with existential questions, I've been different. He left behind a small child and he looked me right in my face and asked me why. We're not equipped with a solid answer for them. All I can tell the deceased is that death is not the end, and usually, most take a few minutes to grieve themselves but then come quietly. This man, however, was more concerned with whom he was leaving behind. And it struck me. Every death that followed felt different to me. But why *did it* affect me so much? It would never have affected any of the other council members. It certainly would not have affected Deacon. It's like in that very moment . . . I *developed* empathy.

My curiosity was piqued. But it wasn't just curiosity that led me to saving Dax. No, back then I knew I was fixing a problem. My scythe had given off a red glow. Azazel had targeted him, and Dax was dying before his date. I was just doing what I thought was right by the council.

But then I fell in love with his sister. *Love.* Not only impossible for a reaper to feel but looked down on. But I also loved Deacon . . . Not in the romantic sense, but I grew fond of her and loved her as a friend. Even if I hadn't realized it. She had been changing too though, I know it. The way she covered for me to the Judge and had helped to save Addison—had she too been developing empathy? Dax's eyes burn into me. He's concerned, but so am I.

"It's not only because Azazel turned me into a human," I finally say. "I had fallen in love with your sister before that. I felt love, empathy. When no other reaper did. Why do you think that is?"

Dax raises a brow and takes a deep breath, spacing out as he contemplates. "Well, I also feel those things."

"Yes, but you became reaper in a different way. You were

a human who died, then became a reaper. The rest of us, we were made this way. I somehow was made different."

"Be happy about that, man. Consider it a gift. You have more insight than anyone else here, and that's how we're going to beat Lorcan. Deacon had a point when she said the Judge's scythe knew what it was doing by choosing you. Having empathy must give you an advantage over the rest of them. Use it."

"Yeah, except I don't even know what I'm doing."

"No one ever really does. But Deacon believed in you. Don't let her death be in vain."

I shrug my shoulders and lean over the podium.

"Are you going to say something?" Dax says.

"Suppose I have to." I shrug. "I just don't know what." Deacon would have been here telling me what to say.

"Maybe just start with how proud you are of the way they fought and haven't abandoned you?"

I raise my eyes. "You're right." You know what . . . ? "Hey, how would you like to be my right hand?"

Dax lifts his right hand and looks at it, staring at me awkwardly. My jaw drops. He isn't this daft. "I'm just kidding. It would be my honor."

A chuckle leaves my mouth and I shake my head. Grabbing the mallet, I hit it on the podium top four times. The chatter quiets and everyone stares at me. I scan the room. Thirty-three reapers left. Thirty-five, including me and Dax, not many at all. "Good, now that I have your attention . . ." I sigh and let go of the mallet. Hollow eyes seer into me and I step down from the podium. "I'd like us all to have a chat, informally."

The reapers swap glances and make a half circle, allowing me to walk into the center of them.

"I know that most of you don't share the mourning for

the loss of Deacon but . . ." My eyes dart from one reaper to the other, trying to see any signs of empathy at all. Forget it, they don't have it. I clear my throat. "Her ability to lead, and her dedication to this council, will surely be missed."

The council of reapers stand beside each other, facing me, blank expressions on their faces. A few of them nod. At least there was something we could agree on. "But on to more serious business. Lorcan has the dagger that controls the demons." Their faces grow grim and rigid. "But he was not able to take my scythe."

One of the reapers steps up from the sidelines. She's a bit shorter than Deacon was but has high cheekbones that make me think of her. "Can he still win, even without the Judge's scythe?"

The council exchanges glances and begins to murmur with one another, concern creasing on their foreheads.

"Not if we work together," Dax interjects.

I take a step toward the reaper who spoke. "What's your name?"

"Clove."

"Clove, that's right," I say. "His army now *is* stronger. He controls the demons, and well, we lost a great many of our councilmen. So, we'll have to be smarter. Quicker. And be three steps ahead of them. We cannot, *will not* let them take LLAPS.

"It feels as though he already has," another reaper says.

"I know it may feel that way. But I am still the Judge, and our power runs through the waters that fill LLAPS.

"There are more of them though, and they have the same access to the waters," Clove says, taking a step forward.

I peer into her. She's right. We are outnumbered. Our strategy needs to be better.

"What about that dragon?" she asks. I part my lips. Evander. He'd gone back to Sidhe. I'm trying not to hate him, but it was his fire that killed Deacon. Sure, it was meant for Lorcan and he used her as a shield, but even still it's hard for me to look at him after that. Especially knowing it was my fault. I was the one who had Evander come into battle as my secret weapon. Orlando had called him, but the rest was my idea. Putting that aside though, the dragons would make a good reinforcement if we can convince them to help.

"For the time being, we cannot count on the dragons to assist us. It is not their fight. For now, let's decide on a course of action that doesn't include the dragons, so that we're not relying on an outside source." All eyes are on me, of course. The council is used to being told what to do, not to be included in any decision making. How did the Judge do it? With Deacon by his side. Maybe he saw her wilfulness, her ability to always do the right thing. Or maybe . . . it was . . . her ability to read thoughts. Did she just always know different courses of action based on what others were thinking? My brows furrow. I hadn't even considered that . . .

Dax takes a seat on the edge of one of the tables, flicking his fire on and off at the tip of his index finger and thumb, lost in thought. Dax recently developed these powers while needing to fight to defend some humans he became fond of. I quirk a brow. I've always been the odd one out of the reapers. I don't even know what the rest of them can do.

"What powers do each of you have?" I ask.

Some of the council furrow their brows, while others screw up their features, looking at one another.

"Well? What can each of you do?"

More silence. What's wrong with them? It's not like they care about personal questions . . . Dax looks up.

"You all do have powers, don't you?" he finally asks. My lips part. I suppose I don't have any power, so some of them might not. But Deacon had. I thought maybe Dax acquired it because he became a reaper differently, but . . . surely some of them would have power. Wouldn't they?

"Umm . . . We don't have any powers," Clove says. I exchange glances with Dax.

"Well, that's peculiar. Were any of you aware that Deacon had telepathy?" A few of them shake their heads, while others nod. OK, some were, some weren't. I wonder if the Judge had any hidden skills.

"None of you are able to do anything . . . extraordinary? Like, Dax can create fire."

"I can catch myself on fire and not feel a thing," he says, a giant grin pasted on his face while he catches his entire right hand on fire.

"What can you do, Ambrose? Can you do anything?" Clove asks.

I pucker my lips. "Afraid not. Which is why at first I thought Deacon was special. Gifted. And that Dax came into a power because he was human first. Not that it makes any sense now, saying it out loud. Humans don't have power." I chafe my chin. "I suppose so much has happened so quickly that I haven't given it much thought. But now that we're discussing it, it is strange that two reapers have powers while the rest of us do not."

"What does it mean?" Clove asks. Yes, what does it mean?

"I'll do my best to find answers. But for now, let's consider our options. What do we know?"

"We know that Lorcan has the dagger." she says. "But you have the scythe."

"We know what he's been up to, collecting souls on Earth," Dax adds.

"Yes." I shift. "He's using them to add to his army, get more powerful. But the question is, why . . . What does he intend to do with all this power? I mean, beside taking over the council and being Judge without the scythe choosing him for the job." He's going through too much trouble just for that. He can come and fight me if he wants to.

Someone in the back clears their throat. "I heard one of the reapers talking before they decided to leave us and join him." I stretch my neck to see who's talking. Reapers turn around and open a gap. He's of middle height and with a round skull-face.

"Yes? And what did they say?"

"They mentioned something about Lorcan wanting to continue Azazel's plans. To unite the planes." Gasps float around the room and I quirk a brow. Why would he want to do that?

"That's good. Your information, that is. What's your name?" I inch forward, cupping my chin.

"My name is Woodrow."

"Thank you, Woodrow. Did they say anything else? Like why they would want to support him in this?" A few reapers laugh.

"Not really, no. But someone else added on to say it would be easier to have total control over the Akashic. I think they meant that reapers would have more control over the planes and on Earth."

I squint my brows at him. "Hmm . . . that'll be true, but by the manner Lorcan is doing it, it'll also give him too much power."

"But you hold the Judge's scythe," Clove says. "Surely, it's more powerful than Lorcan?"

"You would think, but didn't Azazel create both? Would he have made one more powerful than the other?" Dax says.

I shoot him a glance. That's an interesting notion I hadn't considered. If one isn't more powerful than the other, then that makes this scythe a weapon of equal counterpart to the dagger. I should probably keep that to myself in case any more of the council decides to join Lorcan. I don't know how much Lorcan knows about Azazel's weapons.

"That's enough for now. Take a short recess."

Dax stands. "A recess? I thought we were going to discuss strategy . . ."

"Time is running out, Ambrose," Clove says. The pressure of everyone looking at me weighs on my shoulders. This is why people left to join Lorcan's army against me. They don't think I'm fit to lead . . . and if I'm being honest, I don't think I am either. But there's nothing left for me to tell them until I know more.

I'm falling short. I'd hoped that maybe part of this strategy would be to discuss our powers and unite them together. I haven't seen other reapers use them. Shit, does Lorcan have powers? This might work in our favor, actually . . . If Lorcan's army doesn't have power, at least we have Dax on our side. But it isn't enough. Lorcan has demons at his command. I think the only thing I can do here is find answers. I'll have to take a swim inside the Akashic.

"Believe me, I feel the urgency. But rest up. When we meet back in one hour, we will begin training like we did before battling Lorcan's army. We need to stay capable, and you all need your rest."

"What will you do?" Clove asks.

"What the Judge used to do. Confer with the Akashic." That seems to comfort them, and they begin to disperse.

THE STRONGEST POWER

AMBROSE

Conflicted, I stand in the high arched entryway of the Judge's chamber. Technically, these quarters are mine, but it still feels wrong. Like I shouldn't be in here. As if the Judge is going to barge in at any moment and ask me what I'm doing in his own personal quarters. Truth is, I prefer my own quarters. I'm only here to use his Akashic waters.

I slowly stride over to the pond, the serenading pours of the waterfalls easing my tension as I scan the area. His red and gold embellished bed, neatly made just as he left it. His pristine mantle, void of any real personal belongings. But what could any reaper own, really? We only have so many accessories. He did like his fancy bedding and carpet though.

I step down the light stone steps where the pond area is and onto the platform that holds the scrying bowl. The same bowl he used to train Deacon in scrying. I was never trained. And I don't have her here to show me how. Nor to do it for me. Scrying into the universal consciousness is different than using the waters to spy on Earth. I sigh.

A small obsidian ladle hangs by the side. I take it and reach down to the pond, fill it, and pour it into the bowl. I remember seeing her do this a few times until it was filled halfway. I do the same, mimicking the memory.

There, that should do it. Now what? I suppose I have to ask a question. I clear my throat. Right then . . . umm . . . here goes . . . My mind wanders to Addison. I wonder where she is . . . if she's okay. Orlando had come to me with news after the battle, thinking she had come to LLAPS only for us to find out she went to a different dimension. Am I doing the right thing by not going after her? I should probably . . .

"No." She can take care of herself. Deacon would want me to stay put. For the council . . . and I don't have another choice. I shake my head. By defeating Lorcan, I'll also be making it safe for Addison. Orange clouds surface over the bowl and I squint. What's it trying to show me? The clouds disperse and Addison is standing there . . . in her living room! I let out a sigh of relief. She's home and she's okay. That makes it easier to concentrate. Then my frown deepens when I see the horns on her head.

"What have they done to you?" I whisper and wipe my face.

I'll deal with that later. The waters are sensitive. I need to focus on the reapers. "Why do some reapers have powers while others don't?" I finally blurt out.

The clouds turn a dark blue. I lean over the bowl, but the clouds dissipate and all I can see is the reflection of myself. My hollow eyes staring back at me. Maybe that was the wrong question. I'll try again. "Which reapers have powers?" Yes, that should be clearer.

The clouds return, a dark blue again, but this time they disperse easily and show Dax turning his arms into fire, then his head. Good . . . it's working. I don't expect it to show Deacon because she's gone. The clouds disappear over Dax. "Anyone else?" The clouds disperse and I furrow my brows. The reaper it reveals . . . is me. But how? I don't have any powers. This is wrong.

"Water, how can I have powers? What powers do I have?" Images start to pour in . . . of me saving a boy, of saving Dax . . . of me kissing Addison . . . What the hell does that mean? The council and the judge made it very clear to me that this was a hindrance. Empathy and love aren't powers. Are they?

One last question. "What should I do?"

The water clears, replacing the blue clouds with white ones. I wait a few moments and I appear on the surface again. Standing in front of the pond. I watch as I disrobe and step foot into the waters. My jaw drops to my gut. No . . . "But I can't . . . I'll contaminate the water." Even when Deacon brought me back to life, she laid me down on the floor and fed me the water with the ladle. She would never approve of me swimming in it! That's the most taboo thing in LLAPS, apart from falling in love with a human! Well, who better to break that rule than me, I guess?

"No . . ." I shake my head. "This can't be right . . . I won't do it." But the water is never wrong, is it? It's all universal knowledge. The image repeats itself until I watch myself dunk my head inside. I gasp and flick my gaze over to it. It really wants me to step in it? Or did I make this decision myself and it's just showing me my foolish future?

I chafe my chin. I'm no good at this. I step away from the bowl and walk over to the edge of the stone pond. There's only one way to find out, I guess.

Like the image showed, I undo my robes and let them fall to the ground. Dipping one bony, skeletal toe into the cool water, I put one foot inside. And then the other. Well, contamination or not, the damage is done. I might as well complete the task now.

I walk in deeper, fully submerging myself in the universal waters of the Akashic until I'm neck deep. Then, I dunk my head and my whole world changes.

1854 SEVASTOPOL, RUSSIA

The retching sound of vomit jolts me awake. Only seconds —minutes? Hours?—had passed since I had finally fallen asleep. I squint. Even the dim light in the hospital tent is too bright to stand. Instantly, my stomach takes a turn for the worse. I struggle to sit up; my joints ache and I'm too weak to stand on my own. Someone runs over and hands me a bucket. I barely make it in before puking my guts out over the floor. My body convulses as there's nothing else that can come out of me. I've given it all to fertilize the soil already.

The woman gently pushes down on my shoulders till I'm once again lying on my back. She places a wet cloth on my forehead and starts humming, lulling me to sleep. My eyes drift over to the side, landing on the musket that waits for me to get better. Only a matter of days before it gets given to someone able to use it.

It's cold. So cold. My bones shake and the light blanket I have over me does nothing to suppress my chills.

"What about this one?" A man asks the middle-aged nurse who was just tending to me.

"Cholera as well."

"Don't suppose there's any hope? Already looking like a skeleton, he is." There's a pause and then . . .

"Best we pray to God he makes it."

"Ay, we can't lose any more men."

I don't know how long after, but she comes back and holds my hand tight. I drift off to sleep . . . And then . . . the last thing to go was my hearing.

A wave of water rushes over me and I shoot up out of the water. Holy shit. I was a human! My eyes widen and I gasp. Dax, Orlando, even Evander and the owl, Crowley, are standing in front of the pond, watching me. And the hellhound . . .

"Ambrose, what the hell are you doing in there?" Dax shouts, and I can't help but laugh. I start to stand and they all yell for me to stop.

"Woah there, partner . . . Look down."

Huh? Oh! When did I change to human form? My eyes dart over to my robes bundled on the ground. Dax grabs them and hands them to me while everyone turns around. I quickly put them on over my wet skin.

"Decide to go for a swim in the Akashic?" Dax asks. "Is that what Judges do when no one is watching?"

I scrunch up my features. ". . . No. I can explain."

"Relax, I'm just messing. What happened?"

"I came to scry . . . as the Judge and Deacon would do . . . and then . . . the strangest thing happened."

Everyone's brows are raised while I try to find the words . . . "It wanted me to go in . . ."

"Into the waters?" Evander says. I nod. "That's not strange to us. What did you see?"

My eyes widen. Not strange to the dragons? Also, why is

he here? I thought he went back to Sidhe. My eyes flick to Dax.

"Dax! I died around your age! I mean . . . I guess I am your age because I'm dead! I haven't aged!"

Dax's eyes widen, his eyebrows dart up to the top of his head and his lips pucker into an O. I start laughing so hard I almost hurl. "I just experienced myself die for the second time in the most devastating way and for some reason, I cannot stop laughing!"

"Okay . . ." Dax starts. "Just slow down. What are you trying to say?" I grab his shoulders. "I was human! I died of cholera during the Crimean War!" His eyes are now blood-shot and staring at me.

"But . . ."

"Yes! It means all reapers were humans! And the Judge . . ." I let my last word trail as I look down to the side. The Judge was hiding it from us. But why?

"This makes sense," Evander chimes in. "I have heard of this history, but no one speaks about it in Sidhe."

I gape at him. "I must learn more about your history and about what you all know." There's so much I want to find out now. I turn to look at the waters. So much more. About my life and about the reapers . . . About the Judge. Something tells me he was keeping far more secrets than he let on. The hellhound barks and my attention snaps to her.

"There are rumors in Sidhe, age-old rumors, that say the Judge reprogrammed dead humans to be reapers, robotic in nature." He shrugs. "But that was way before my time."

I exchange glances with Dax. "The waters told me some-thing else."

"What?" they all say.

"Apparently . . ." I lower my voice. If I'm honest, I'm a

little embarrassed by this . . . "My empathy *is* my power." No one says a word. "I know. Kind of lame, isn't it?"

"Not at all," Orlando says. "Not one bit. It makes you the strongest yet." I offer him a smile.

"Wait, so does that mean . . . the other reapers . . . ?" Dax scratches at his temple and I nod, grinning.

"I believe they can all develop their powers. We just have to find out how."

"That's great," Dax says solemnly, and I squint at him. "Guess that means we have our second task then."

"Second?" I dart over to the rest of them. "Why are you all here, anyway?" Evander takes a step forward.

"I came to warn of a problem. Lucifer contaminating the waters of HAPS and now HAPS' angels are looking to raid Sidhe. I came down asking for help when . . ."

"When an influx of newly contracted demons came down to LLAPS under Lorcan's command. We think they're due to Lorcan's human-killing spree to unite the planes," Orlando finishes for Evander in one breath.

FREAKING ZOMBIES!?

ADDISON

Wind tousles my hair as the portal vents close behind me.

Expecting the gray stone flooring and high gothic arches of LLAPS' narrow corridors, I pause to the familiar smell of books and soft light gleaming in through the window of my library. "Well, this isn't LLAPS . . ." Why am I here?

My muscles ease. I hadn't realized I had been tensing them before barging back into LLAPS to pick a very unprepared fight with Lorcan. Not that I'm complaining, but seriously, how did I end up back home? I wasn't focusing on my house . . . My eyes fall to the couch where my father had been lying the last time I was here. He's not here now though . . . Where is he?

"Dad?" I call out, walking to the intercom to try and reach the rooms of the rest of the house. I hold down the green button and call out his name a few times, but no one responds, just static. My gut clenches. I really hope he's here somewhere and did not walk into LLAPS in his physical body. But knowing my dad, if he came back in his spirit form not having found me out there and no signs of me here, he probably did go back out there.

More reason for me needing to go back to LLAPS. Plan or no plan, I need to hurry back there. I can beat Lorcan. He has my dagger, mine being the keyword. And it's my power, not his. I'm stronger . . . *Keep telling yourself that, Addie.* But he hasn't gone through the transformation I have, so it must be true. I turn back around and try the hidden door that leads to the astral realm.

Locked.

I screw up my face, turn around, and reach for the button on the podium. No clicking sounds? I try the door again. Still locked. The wardings I protected the house with wouldn't lock *me* out . . . Did my dad come back, lock it, then leave again? Why would he do that? I wave my hand in a circular motion to release any locks he may have put and try again. Nope. I'm completely locked out. My magick should have worked there . . . Strange. And also . . . crap! I have twenty-four hours to get to LLAPS and make things right. My heart pounds. That's not enough time. What was I thinking?

I was thinking I had no other choice.

I squeeze my eyes shut. *Mom, if you can hear me . . . I need more time.* Doubt that'll work though.

I walk over to the family room where there's more space and hold my hand out in front of me. What should I focus on? All the images surfacing from my memories of that place come back—gross. How about I focus on one of the corridors I had been in before, a safe one, without nasty hellish silverfish?

My hand tingles. A portal spins open. Yes! And just as I take a step forward, it closes.

What the hell? Ever since my transformation in the in-between, I haven't needed to focus so hard on my magick. I opened a portal from that dimension to HAPS for Pete's sake, I should be able to open one to LLAPS. I mean, I'm a demon after all, aren't I? I hold my hand out again, trying the same thing. This time the portal flashes once and then closes. I squint one eye. Huh. Could it be that I'm low in energy? My stomach grumbles. Self-doubt permeates my thoughts while I make my way to the kitchen. I guess it makes sense, but . . . I've been without food for hours since Padrino's . . . I swallow. I had almost forgotten about him. I had something to drink at HAPS . . . and I was fine. Not to mention not having eaten while I was in the Lower Astral Planes. And that still didn't stop me from transforming myself into a demon, coming into my power, and opening portals. So why now?

I grab the moka pot on the dish rack and open it. Doesn't mean I don't want food right now and that I can't enjoy some coffee . . . I open the tap and reel back. Brown water and gunk spit out from the faucet. Yuck! I quickly close it. What's going on? Okay, well . . . no coffee then. I open cabinets looking for something to eat. Anything that doesn't involve actual cooking. I find a bag of potato chips and some bread and jam. The power still isn't working, so the fridge will be disgusting. Not opening that. Which also means . . . things must be bad outside. I mean, if there's gunk coming out of the faucet? Real bad.

I set the jam and bread on the table, turn around, and open the cabinet where we keep the plates. I pull one out and turn to set it next to the . . . Where'd the jam go? I raise a brow. Um . . . I know I just set this down on the glass table. I set the plate down and turn toward the kitchen island. And there on the top is the jam. I—uh, maybe I do need to eat. I take the jam and set it down next to the plate. I need a knife.

I make my way over to the drawer next to the sink and pull out a knife. When I get back to the table, I take a seat and reach for the . . . Where'd the bread go? What the hell is going on? I get up, knocking my leg on the glass edge, and scan the kitchen. Over by the far end of the adjacent table to the island, next to the fridge and cooking books, is the dang bread. Okay . . . I did not put it over there. I scamper over to it and grab it in a fury.

"Whatever spirits are here fucking with me, I am *not* in the mood." The last time I dealt with a mischievous little ghost was my own brother. But that's when I was under that memory curse and I didn't recognize Dax or the younger ghost version of himself. My father had been dreaming up Dax when he was a child and since he was cursed and his dreams were leaking out due to a demon feeding off him, some of his dreams would come out to play . . . as ghosts. Fun times. But anyway, I'm hungry.

I take a seat and stuff my face until I'm full.

Okay, let's try again. I stand up and go back to the living room. I stick my hand out and attempt to open the portal. A flash of light zips in and then goes out. Seriously, what the hell? One more time. I hold out my hand. Zip.

"Ugh!" What do I do? It's not like I can even call Dax with a cell phone. Shit. Is it because I need to sleep? But I'm not tired. I did fall asleep in the cave. Mind you, it was a disrupted sleep, but I got to rest. And I'm all hyped up—no, I'm not tired. It's not that. I start pacing back and forth in front of the fireplace.

A low growl comes from behind me. I spin around, half-expecting to see Skadi, my hellhound, prowling on an egregore, but my eyes land on the empty family room. Nothing hangs from the three-tier chandelier nor is there anything chewing up the couches. I scan the picture frames on the table and look up to the empty door of my bedroom. Nothing. Hmm . . . strange. Turning back, I extend my arm out again for lack of anything better to try. One more time won't hurt, right? A louder, more ravenous growl comes from what I'm assuming is outside. I make a beeline to the window, glad that whatever it is isn't inside the house. It is *not* going to be that kind of party! Not in my house again, not with the wardings I put in place.

I peer out to my father's car and almost have a heart attack to find that my car isn't there. That's right, I left it at Ava's. I start down the stairs for a better look because it's hard to see if someone (or a demon) is just outside the door from over the overlapping roof of the second floor. The growl turns into a long moan and I slow my step as I near the downstairs window on the other side of the stairwell.

"Oh, hell no . . ." I gasp.

A man . . . a *dead* man stands with his scruffy brown hair pressed to the window as he moans, saliva dripping out of his mouth.

Is that a freaking zombie!? You've got to be kidding me. I knew things here had gotten bad but . . . How is this even possible? Last time Dax and I were here, demons were collecting souls . . . How are dead people walking around, soulless? I rush to the door and unlock it, stepping into the humid Florida air. I pause. It's humid again . . . which means . . . LLAPS's portals are closed. That's a good thing but . . . then why are there zombies?

The zombie arches up, his blank stare now focused on me as he begins to walk. Anyone else would run back inside and lock the doors—hell, they wouldn't have opened the door to begin with. But, that's anybody else. I'm me and I have demon powers. I'll be damned if I allow zombies to roam my town! Holding out a hand, electrical power surges through my fingertips, stunning the zombie. An aroma of burnt human flesh soon assaults my nostrils and I swallow my gag reflexes. I take my hand away as the zombie drops to the ground. I search the area. No other zombies around, I wonder who and why this guy was to make it through my gate. I had put a warding against demons before leaving but nothing against humans. I guess since zombies are technically dead humans, my warding doesn't apply to them. Welp, it will now. I jog over to the gate and bring the iron in. They clank as I push down the iron bar into the hole on the pavement. The lock clicks and I step away, drawing out both arms and envisioning a protective ward against all humans, zombies, or paranormal hooligans. As far as anyone is concerned, this house doesn't exist on this street and lies within a pocket dimension.

I slam the door shut behind me and make it back upstairs. Okay. Three things I've learned. One, there are zombies walking around Tavernier Key. Two, I cannot open a portal. And three, it has nothing to do with my powers. So, what gives?

I make my way up to my bedroom and sit on the edge of the bed until I notice the black dirt on the bottoms of my jeans. Gross. Suddenly, I'm a thankful that I did come back home. I got so used to my cloak weighing me down that I forgot I had it on. I undress and take my phone out of my pocket. Uh oh . . . I try turning it on, but it's dead. Plugging it into the charger, I squeeze my eyes shut hoping it'll still charge. Let's see . . . Since the last time I used it to talk to Ava, I escaped revitalizers, fought guardsmen and reapers, saved prisoners, and oh yeah, fell into the Akashic river in HAPS. Nope, it's broken. I chuck it on the bed. Honestly, I'm surprised it didn't break sooner.

When I'm about to turn on the shower, I remember the nasty water that came out of the sink. Shall I dare?

Grimacing, I turn the knob. When clear water spouts out, I let out a sigh of relief. The one good thing about living in a mansion is there are multiple pipes running through the house. Something must be clogging the kitchen pipes. My stomach turns at the thought of seeing the zombie. Hopefully, it isn't a dead body.

I grab the shampoo and pour a bit into the palm of my hand. When I set it down and start lathering my hair, the bottle floats on its own and sets itself down next to the faucet. I swallow and look from side to side. Okay, I just put a double warding over the house, there's no way that can be a ghost.

"Hello?" I say. My stomach gives a little flutter, and it brings me back to the thing I've been avoiding, the undeniable truth that there's a demon baby inside of me. I start scrubbing myself clean and picking up the pace. Maybe there's something in the library that can tell me why the portal isn't opening. Could I be blocked? I gasp. Could Lorcan have blocked me out? If that's true, then LLAPS would be under siege . . .

I dry myself up and go back to my room to pick out an outfit. I'm planning on going into battle, so this time I want to be better prepared and not end up with soaked jeans and generally uncomfortable.

Humming to myself, I take out a sports bra and sporty pants with zippers that turn into shorts because, hello, two outfits in one? Especially when I might possibly end up in contaminated water again? No brainer. I quickly slip on my clothes and dry off my hair with my towel. I reach for my brush and start untangling the knots while staring at my reflection in my vanity mirror. It's been a long time since I've felt clean. So much better.

I keep humming "Stairway to Heaven" because it's what my brother likes to play on the guitar. I miss him, okay?

My stomach jumps and I jolt. I stop singing. *Was that you again?* Do you like my singing? I continue the tune and I lift my shirt above my belly. I hardly even see a little bump; it's only been a couple of weeks. It can't be kicking so soon . . . Right? Although, who knows what a demon spawn is capable of . . . I set the brush down and reach for a hair tie in my dresser drawer. Putting it on my wrist, I separate my hair into three strands. While I sing, and reach for my brush when . . . my brush flies across the room. Uhhh . . . I walk over to the corner next to the door and pick it up again. With eyebrow quirked, I quietly brush my strands to tightly braid them, tying it tight with my hair tie. I stick my brush in the drawer and gasp at my reflection. My braid is floating behind me. Like Pippy Long Stockings but with just one braid. My tummy jumps.

I gasp. "Are you doing this?" This little demon baby has powers . . . Already? But . . . isn't that impossible? I am in over my head with this. My bedroom door shuts and then opens. I gape at it. I lift my shirt again and stare at the mirror. My eyes widen as I watch in horror as my stomach moves, forming bumps until it forms the image of a tiny face with horns. Then disappears. "Oh!" I shoot back. My hair drops down and the door slightly opens, creaking as it does.

I shut my mouth. Something tells me this is not going to be a normal pregnancy . . . unless I take the potion my mother gave me. But one thing's for sure: I can't ignore it anymore. Either way, taking the potion will have to wait until I defeat Lorcan. I need my powers for this.

I grab some combat boots out of my closet and put them

on. I have no idea how I'm going to get the portal to open, but I'm hoping there's a spell somewhere in the library that can tell me about breaching wards. And just maybe, I can tweak it to sneak into LLAPS.

I shuffle through spell books, tossing aside old dragon mythology and anything that will be zero help for me in there. My father, of all things, is a collector. Interesting stuff? Yes. But annoyingly, he doesn't like to keep them organized.

Something clicks and my eyes flick over to the hidden door that leads to my father's pocket dimension. How did that open? I tried that already and I was locked out. My stomach makes a move. *Was that you?* The thought of that sends a shiver down my spine. Just how much can this baby understand? Okay, get it together. Twenty-four hours, remember!

I make my way back to the portal door, take a deep breath, and walk inside. As the door shuts behind me, I make this quicker by trying to open a portal. I don't need to go to my dad's pocket dimension, and I certainly don't want to go wandering off into the dark abyss. Immediately, a portal opens when I stick my hand out. I'm not sure why I was having a hard time before, but something tells me my unborn demon baby's power next to mine has something to do with it. This'll be fun.

Next up, LLAPS.

A DEMONIC REUNION

ADDISON

step a foot onto the stone corridor of LLAPS, and before the portal even closes, I'm blinded by fire. I scream as my wings bust open from my back. What the hell? Do they just come out when they want? I crouch low on the ground, shielded by my wings. The smell of burnt feather tickles my nose and my breath hitches. I'm going to be burnt alive!

"Hey!" I yell and stumble back, trying to see through the flames. Wait a minute, I have elemental power. As I will it, water emerges from the walls and the ground, in waterfalls. And this is why I didn't wear jeans.

Slowly, I stand up straight, ready to face whatever fire demon attacked me. With my wings still covering my body, I peek through them, enough to see ... Oh ... my ... god ... My knees tremble. Right in front of me stands a ... a fucking dragon.

Dragons are real? I start to backpedal, but the dragon lets out another surge of fire and I quickly counteract with a water blast from my hands. Steam singes my surroundings and the dragon backs up and winces, its flame dampening. I take a step forward and let out another blast. The dragon shakes its head and groans.

"What? Don't like water?"

The dragon gives off a quick shake than a tremor before it starts to minimize in size. Uhh . . . is it shrinking? The dragon minimizes to around my height and I lift my chin. Yep, definitely shrinking. I gasp as a bright light surfaces around it, momentarily blinding me until it has shifted into a woman. Woah.

The lights snuffs out. She has medium length blonde hair pulled back into a ponytail with two twisted, iridescent, white horns coming from her head. She's wearing a tight, dark-green tunic that passes her tight brown leggings. She raises her chin, her eyes boring into me. She's drenched, and frowning. For a moment we both stare at each other, unmoving. I mean, what am I supposed to do? I just watched a dragon shift into a human. I'm both excited and freaked out!

"... Hi ..." I start.

"Don't you make another move, demon," she snaps. Demon? "How did you get past the barriers?" Barriers? Oh, that's why I couldn't open a portal into LLAPS . . .

"I'm not a demon, I mean . . . I am, but . . . not entirely . . ."

"Answer the question." She puffs smoke from her nostrils, and I put my hands up. Oh, I really don't have time for this.

"Woah there, smoky, let's all calm down." Unless you want another blast of water. "I'm not sure how I got past the barriers," I lie. "I just did." She comes closer, her eyes fixated on me, studying my face.

"So . . . dragons are real . . ."

She grimaces and reaches to the back of her belt,

unlatching a pair of handcuffs. "Shut up and don't move." My mouth parts.

"Yeah, no. You're not putting those on me. Listen . . ."

"I said shut up." She mutters a few words in a language I've never heard and runes appear on the handcuffs, glowing bright yellow.

"Yeah, I'm still not letting you put those on m—" The cuffs appear on my wrists on their own. She didn't even have to get close to me. And they come with a metal link chain connected to her. Great. "Oh, what the hell, man?"

"Why is it so hard for you to keep quiet? I said no talking."

"Are you part of Lorcan's army?" I blurt out. She takes an aggressive step forward. "Alright, alright, I won't speak. Jeesh."

She turns on her heel and starts down the dark corridor, yanking me along. "And no, I am not a part of Lorcan's traitors. I'm taking you straight to the Judge." My eyes flicker.

". . . The Judge? Which Judge?"

She turns her head. "Boy, you're really lost, aren't you? The reaper Ambrose is the new Judge of LLAPS. He'll say what to do with a demon like you." My stomach does a somersault. Oh my god. She's taking me to see Ambrose. I don't know why I thought I could come down here and fight off Lorcan, hopefully find my brother, but avoid dealing with Ambrose. I mean . . . I guess I knew he'd fall into the equation at some point . . . it's just that . . . He had put a freaking APB on me. And now I'm a prisoner? My rage fights my excitement to see him.

"Oh, so now you're quiet? Good. You should be scared. Ambrose is a fearless leader. He'll wonder why I didn't kill you myself."

Fearless leader, huh? Looks like he's taken his new role seriously. "Why didn't you kill me?"

"Dragon fire is the only thing that can permanently kill an immortal. The moment you started speaking, I knew you were a high-level demon. You're part of Lorcan's army and we want answers."

"Wait . . ." I chuckle. "You think I'm part of Lorcan's army?" I sigh.

"No tricks, demon!" she hisses. "Shows how lost you are, asking a dragon from Sidhe if she's part of his army. Don't you know your own?"

"No, this is all one big misunderstanding. Let me go and I'll explain. I know Ambrose . . ."

"I've heard enough. Be silent the rest of the way." Jeesh, she's uptight. She walks a brisk pace, the chain pulling me along with every step. The corridors become lighter as she leads me down a different pathway. The arches become wider, showcasing the rest of the realm. I look over to my right at the tall gothic-style windows overlooking the mountain region of LLAPS' labyrinth. Dragons circle the purple-hazed sky, guarding any portals that may or may not open. My eyes skim the hall for demons, loose prisoners, burnt ones, anything. But there's nothing. The corridors are clean, or at least this one is. Maybe it's because we're in the reaper's quarters now. I try to listen out for guardsmen, but all I hear is the flapping of wings from the dragons patrolling above. It's not that I'm not used to LLAPS being eerie, but this just feels weird.

"Ahem . . ." I say.

"What part of 'I want you to be silent the rest of the way' do you not understand?"

"Sorry. I'm just wondering . . . where is everyone?"

She makes a full stop and I nearly bump into her. "Everyone?"

"Yeah, you know . . . all the guards . . . revitalizers . . . other escapees . . ."

"As if you don't know, demon. Come on, hurry up. We're almost there." She tugs on the chain and I almost trip over my own boots. Guess that means Lorcan has taken them, too? Well, I know escapees went to Earth, but I know some were roaming around here. Guess Ambrose had those all collected.

"So, how come there are dragons?" I say, knowing I'm just pissing her off. We pass by another high-arched window and a black dragon with red streaks of hair in its coat swoops down only to fly up again.

"None of your business."

Nice. "What's your name?"

"Also none of your business." She's great at making conversation.

"I'm Addison."

"I don't care."

"But people call me Addie."

"Still don't care."

"Also . . . not really a demon."

She huffs. "As if you don't reek of one."

What the . . . ? "Hey, I don't smell. You smell."

"I probably smell like a dragon. Like you smell like a demon."

"Not that I mind it. Just like I don't mind the smell of a clean dog."

"Are you calling me a dog? And I said no talking!"

"No—I . . ." Forget it. I guess my mom was right about the trail demons leave behind.

She stops in front of a high-arched doorway and the

crashing of waterfalls come from the other side. "We're here." I gulp. I'm not ready to see Ambrose. I'm . . . different now. And so is he. What's he even going to do to me? Has he really changed that much? Is he like this dragon says he is? Some ruthless, fearless leader—head of the Reaper Council? Is he as soulless as Deacon was when I first met her? Is he going to . . . imprison me? Or kill me? I suck in a breath as she knocks on the door three times. I wince and the door opens.

She yanks at my chains and brings me inside.

"Warning, I have a demon in my chains. She's somehow strong enough to bypass your wards, so she's higher-level. Thought you'd want to question her. Or, I could stick her in one of the cages till you get around to it? Your choice, I just thought she might have some immediate information on Lorcan."

My eyes raise to the swarm of reapers gathering around the cathedral-like ceilings of a closed waterfall area. Massive and breathtaking. I had forgotten how beautiful some areas of LLAPS are. Reapers move away, some widening their eyes at me. Do they recognize me from when I released Lucifer? Oh, I'm definitely not wanted here.

They spread out, making way. In the far end Ambrose stands, clutching his golden scythe.

"Release her."

"But—"

"Blaise, release her at once." I look at Blaise and slant my smile. I'm not gonna lie, I'm relieved to know he isn't going to kill me.

"See? Told ya." She grunts and mutters a few words. My cuffs break loose, and she latches them back onto her belt.

"Addison—" His breath hitches and he dashes for me. I take a step back, rotating my wrists.

"So, you know this demon?"

"She's not a—" His eyes stop at my horns and he grimaces. "She's my—" His eyes land on my lips and back to my eyes. I'm his what?

"Addie!" a familiar voice calls out from the side lines.

I flick my eyes over to see Dax running at me. Next to him is Skadi and my father with Crowley perched on his head. My eyes burn, blurring with tears. I run into my brother's arms and he lifts me up.

"Where did you go?" he says, setting me down gently.

"Long story. We have a lot to catch up on." I turn to my dad.

"I cannot believe you're here . . . I mean, I knew you were, but I can't believe you followed me!"

"Of course I did." I give him a big hug and pat Crowley on his head before scratching an overly excited hellhound behind the ears.

"Oh, Skadi! I can't believe I'm saying this, but I've missed you too!"

"She's Crowley's new best friend now." Dax pats Crowley on his feathers. I chuckle as Crowley huffs and turns his back around.

"Oh yeah, I'm sure they are," I say. I turn back to Ambrose. His expression is somber as he hasn't taken his eyes off me. My chest tightens. What he must think of me right now.

"Addie . . ." My dad's voice quakes. And I know he's thinking it too. He hasn't seen my horns until now. My face reddens.

"Dad . . . Let's not interrogate her . . ." Dax says.

"Okay, stop." I might as well get this over with. "Yes, I turned into a demon and I have new powers. But I am here for one purpose only, and that's to get Earth back to normal. And I have twenty-four hours to do it."

"What? Why twenty-four hours?" Ambrose asks. I explain all that I went through getting to HAPS and how Lucifer poisoned the Akashic waters and my mother's threat to send down the Angel Army.

"You saw Mom?" Dax's voice quivers.

"Yeah, she looks great. She's some kind of general now, it seems." Ambrose widens his eyes and exchanges glances with a tall man with iridescent horns on his head. Another dragon shifter?

"That is not good news," the man says. "HAPS is relentless and brutal. We need to act fast."

"And who are you?"

"This is Evander," Dax cuts in. "Dad's friend."

"Ah, nice to meet you and agreed. I'm not sticking around, and I'm definitely not taking up the mantle to become some demon queen." Dax and my dad exchange glances, I refuse to look at Ambrose, though his eyes sear into me. Murmurs from between the reapers and the few dragon shifters that are around erupt.

"Well," Dax breaks the silence, "we're all here. Let's catch you up to speed. HAPS army or not, strategy comes first."

I meet Ambrose's gaze as Dax starts explaining to me how Evander helped them defeat Lorcan in their battle but went sour when—

"Hmm?" My eyes snap back to him. "Deacon is gone?"

Ambrose gives a nod and drops his gaze down to the floor. Wow. Like, permanently gone? Dust? "I–I'm so sorry, Ambrose."

"Thank you."

"A lot has happened, Addie." My eyes flick over to my

brother. "In fact, we think we may have found an advantage against Lorcan. Ambrose . . . he—"

"I think I'd like a moment alone with Addison," Ambrose interrupts him before he can go any further. "Dax, keep training everyone, but don't start them with the waters yet. Wait for me to come back." Ambrose turns to me. "That is . . . if that's okay with you?" He says, bringing his voice down to a whisper. How can I say no? This is long overdue. I nod and take his hand. The dragon who had chained me gapes.

"Can someone please explain to me what is going on?" she says.

"Yeah, come on, Blaise. I'll tell you everything." Dax motions for her to follow him. Ambrose pulls me gently to the side of the room toward the waterfalls. Skadi barks and trails after us.

"Skadi!" Dax calls out. She looks at him, then back at me.

"I'll be right back, Skadi," I say, and she runs off toward Dax. It always amazes me just how much more hellhounds can understand compared to our dogs back on Earth. The crashing sounds of the water hitting the surface of the pond get louder as Ambrose leads me up some stone steps, overlooking the reapers who are training.

"We'll get some privacy up here."

"Mhmm . . ."

We walk up to a stone platform with a red carpet, pillows, and throws around a central area. This is the first time I've seen any kind of accessory decorating LLAPS that isn't fake. The last time beautiful garments appeared to me was in the mental plane when . . . Azazel had a glamour on to make himself look and sound like Ambrose. Only to . . . Ugh. I shake the memory out of my head and sigh deeply.

"Addison," Ambrose starts. "I am so sorry . . ."

My eyes flick to his. They're sulking and wet. He, unlike the rest of the Reaper Council, apart from my brother, is in his human form.

"I thought you'd be . . . skeletal, or something," I say.

He flinches. "I was, but recently, I made it my choice to not have to change. That was the old Judge who wanted reapers to be skeletal and distant. But, I made a discovery that leads me to believe this is better."

"What recent discovery?"

"Later." He takes my other hand and holds them both tight.

"Well, I agree." I smile.

"Addison, I—"

"Yeah, I know, you're sorry. I get it." I release my hands from his grip and his frown deepens.

"I know you're upset with me. You have to know that I did not know you had turned into . . . "

"A demon? You can say it. I turned into a demon." His mouth snaps shut, and he looks disgusted.

"This isn't your fault," he says. "Deacon lied to me. And she forced your brother to lie to you too. You shouldn't be mad at him."

My face slackens. "I know. And I'm not, anymore. And— I know you didn't mean to put an APB on my head." His face brightens. "It's okay, really. To be honest, I've come into my powers now."

"What does that mean?"

"It means, it is what it is. I have demon blood in me, Azazel made me reach my highest potential." He twists his face up as he searches my features. "No, don't get it twisted. I hate him. With a passion." If only you knew what he did to me. "But, I am more powerful now and I'm starting to understand that demons were handed the bad end of the stick." Hearing myself say this out loud makes me rethink taking the potion. I have come into my powers—do I really want to give them up?

Ambrose's face twists again. Oh yeah, idioms. "What I mean is, their lives haven't been fair, for centuries. And it's not their fault they are the way they are. They're misunderstood, is all I'm saying."

He licks his lips. "I understand. But I still need to bring them back down."

"Oh, totally. I agree they do not belong on Earth. But I don't agree with them being annihilated."

"No, you're right. I have changed courses. Especially after the dragons showed up and I found out about—"

"Speaking of that," I cut him off. I'm tired of hearing about me. "What's with the dragons?"

"Lorcan had sent an influx of demons under his influence to try to take siege of LLAPS. Some of them were ripped from their mortal bodies, leaving the humans . . . In a strange state of being . . ."

"The zombies."

"What?"

"A human without a spirit . . . empty but hungry for flesh . . ." I say.

"Yes, that would be a possibility. Did you see a zombie?" I purse my lips and nod. Nothing surprises me anymore.

"The only way to fix LLAPS and Earth is to make sure no one gets in, no one gets out. The dragons are helping to secure the portals."

"Isolate the problem."

"Yes." Makes sense. An awkward silence closes in on us.

Only the sounds of the water falling and the reapers training below permeate the space. He looks down at my lips and my heart starts to thunder.

"Oh, Addison." He grabs the back of my head and draws me in. His lips crash against mine and for a moment I welcome it. My eyes part and take in the way his strong jaw curves, his lashes, his skin . . . His face morphing into Azazel flashes in my mind. I gasp and push him away.

"What's wrong?"

"I'm sorry Ambrose . . . I can't." It's too much. Will I ever get that image out of my head? My stomach flutters and I hold onto my belly. His eyes drop down to my stomach. Does he know?

"Can't what? Addie . . . Tell me." I see the pain in his eyes and my breath shallows. I spent such a long and heart-breaking time trying to find him, only to be deceived and watch him die, and now I finally have him back and I don't want to be with him? What is wrong with me?

"I don't know." I grab onto my hair.

"If it's because you're a demon now, Addison, I don't care." My heart skips a beat. Hearing him say he doesn't care, I am what I am in a good way . . . is good news, I guess.

"Why don't you care?" I know I'm pushing things, but I have to know.

"Because I love you, Addison. And like you say, I believe you. I believe not all demons are bad. And I trust you."

"Why do you love me? We weren't even together for that long."

"You're right, but it was different for me. You awoke feelings in me I didn't know were there. You were the only person I ever thought about. While I was human . . . I was scared for you. Worried about you. I was worried that if I lost my memory, I would forget you. And that was the scariest thing out of all that had happened to me."

My gut clenches and tears well up in my eyes. I did love him too. Maybe I still do . . . but I can't look at him and not see Azazel emerging from out of his skin. And besides . . . I hold on to my stomach tighter. Would he even want to raise Azazel's kid?

"Addie, I—" He sighs. "I know." My eyes flick up at him.

"What do you know, exactly?" He places his hand on my stomach.

"I know . . ." Oh . . .

"How?" It doesn't really matter how he found out. He's a reaper—a Judge with Akashic insight. Plus, I'm sure someone would have told him.

"Don't worry about how I found out. Just know that . . . I am so sorry for how this happened to you. And . . . it doesn't change anything." My lips part. Why is he so caring? Soulless reapers? I know humans worse than them. This has to be the kindest thing I've ever heard.

"But . . . it's a demon . . . Ambrose . . . and . . ." A tear falls down my face. He wipes it away and lifts my chin.

"And?"

"It's only been a few weeks and it's showing some serious powers."

"Yes. Unborn demon offspring not only show signs of their power early on, but they cannot be killed. You're carrying an immortal child." I hadn't thought of it in that way. I'm carrying an *immortal child.*

"I used to be human," he blurts.

"Yes, I know . . . Azazel turned you human. You died in my arms . . ." How could I ever forget?

"No, I mean before that. Long before."

My mother's words come back to me. *The reapers were once human.*

He steps back and turns to stare down at the reapers who have now partnered up and are sparring amongst themselves. He pauses for a moment and begins to tell me how he decided to walk into the pond. He told me of his memory and how he died in the Crimean War. He was a British soldier.

After a few moments of letting him talk, I sigh. "My mother told me. Not about when you were alive but about how every single reaper here was once a human."

He drops his shoulders and nods. "Did she mention anything else about us?"

I shake my head.

My breath trembles. "When will my brother lose his memory?"

"I'm not sure that he will."

Oh? "Why not?"

Ambrose sighs. "I have reason to believe that the Judge wiped our memories away, or rather, had the power to take them and release them into the Akashic. Memories are synapses of energy, you see . . . Difficult to turn to dust just by themselves, so he hid them away."

"In the Akashic."

"Yes."

"But he knew Dax . . . Why didn't he just take his memory then and there? He could have said it was a caveat to him becoming a reaper."

"Dax wouldn't have done it. And the Judge was protective of his secret. He didn't want reapers finding out they were once human."

"That's so weird. Why do you think he did that?"

"That I have yet to find out, but I'm working on it."

"Looks like you have your hands full."

He presses his lips together.

". . . And so do I, Ambrose. I'm sorry . . . I'm trying to envision us together again, but . . . when I look at you, all I see is . . . Azazel." He scrunches his features.

"What? Why?" Oh, clearly he doesn't know all the details. I pinch my nose and tell him everything. Ambrose's face pales, if it could get any paler. I can guess at what he's thinking. That *that's* not how he wanted our first time to be remembered. How he would do anything in his power to turn back time . . . I know.

"I'll fucking *kill* him."

I gulp. It's rare that Ambrose curses. I'm usually the one with the potty mouth. But when he does . . . Holy shit. He could snuff the oxygen out of the room.

"Look . . ." I start. "It's not that I don't want to be with you. I just need some time." To figure shit out and to decide if I can have a relationship with him. It's not only that I see Azazel whenever I see him, it's something else too. He never came when I needed him the most. "Also, even after you found out about me, you watched me from behind the veil and didn't say anything to me. I needed you." He had assumed his position as Judge, and I get that. But he made his choice. "What if something else drastic happens and you decide to ghost me again?"

He momentarily screws up his face. I know it was because I said "ghosted," but then his features soften, and he nods. "You're right. It was the wrong choice. I should have handled it better. I should have been there for you."

"How do I know you wouldn't do it again? How do I know you'll be there for me next time if shit hits the fan?" His brows furrow. I really need to stop using idioms around him. I clear my throat. "If there is a crisis in the future, how do I know you won't ignore me in order to be there for the reapers, instead of me?" I clarify.

"Oh . . . I–I don't know . . ." Comforting. Just what I wanted to hear.

"I need some space to think." I cross my arms and take a step back.

"Ambrose!" Dax calls out, running up the stairs. We both turn to look at him, with the tall dragon dude following behind. "Evander just alerted us that there's been a demon sighting in a city with unharmed humans."

"There are unharmed humans?" I say.

"Yes, Key West hadn't been hit yet—I mean no guards, no revitalizers, no prisoners or demons. Just people living their daily lives. Until now. There are two demons fighting with each other. We have to go *now*."

FIREBALL WITH A SIDE OF ATTITUDE

ADDISON

*A*mbrose and I exchange glances. Did he just say there are two demons fighting with each other in the middle of Key West, *with people around*? Oh my god. We follow Dax and Evander back down to the rest of the Reaper Council. I can't let more people get hurt.

Ambrose makes his way to the front of the group. I stand back next to Dax and my father. The dragon shifters line up behind Ambrose. Blaise stands next to Ambrose, her eyes scanning the room. She stops when she gets to me. Chatter erupts among the reapers.

"Silence," Dax shouts from beside me, and I snort. "Addie, come on."

"Sorry."

Ambrose clears his throat. "There's been a disruption up on Earth. Evander, fill us in on all the details." The dragon shifter takes a step forward.

"This is most likely Lorcan's plot; it seems that demons are under his control as in they cannot think for themselves, under some sort of hypnosis." Reapers in the crowd gasp at the same time and look at one another. Jeez, *Children of the Corn* much?

"That makes sense," I say. Reapers stop to face me in unison, and I try my best to avoid their stares. "He has the dagger and it's meant to control demons . . . by taking away their free will." Some snap their attention back to the front while others continue to stare me down. I try my hardest to ignore them. Something about a room full of skeletons in black cloaks, appalled at me speaking, totally creeps me out. Or at least I think they're appalled? I can't tell by their expressions, but one of them furrowed their brows so deep when I spoke that I'm sure it was out of disgust. I get it. They all hate demons. Whatever.

"If Lorcan is there now, we need to go to him." To my surprise, the reaper with the furrowed brows speaks up.

"You're not ready," Ambrose says.

"But the humans; we can fix this at the same time," she says.

"It's a pretty nasty demon fight by the looks of it," Evander interjects. "But Ambrose is right. You're outnumbered and not strong enough to defeat Lorcan and his demon and reaper union army."

"So, what do we do then? Stay here and sit?"

"No, Clove," Dax says. "You stay here and train." Ah, the furrowing brow reaper has a name!

"But we've been training for days! This is only going to get worse."

I clear my throat and others stop to look at me. "Umm . . . You know, the dagger can also kill immortals such as yourselves. I learned this from Azazel. It's meant to control all LLAPS. Even if he didn't specifically say reapers, he meant you too. Which means he can also control you." I pause. "In the same way he's controlling the demons." Now all the reapers erupt in conversation.

"How would she know this?" one of the skeletal clones says.

"She's one of them. A demon queen. She was fraternizing with Azazel," Clove spews.

And there it is. I ball my fist. Why, that dumb reaper bitch! "Fraternizing?" Power surges down my arm.

"Enough!" Ambrose shouts. Everyone shuts up and I diminish my power. Damn, you go, Ambrose.

Evander and Blaise whisper amongst each other before he steps up. "Ambrose and Dax need to stay here." He turns to Ambrose. "You need to tell them what you saw and how they need to properly train." Ambrose nods.

"Blaise and I will go handle the demon fight."

"Right," Ambrose continues. "We split up, then."

Evander nudges him. "Go on." Ambrose mutters thanks and takes a moment to scan the room. "There's something I want to speak to you about before we begin. Yesterday, after I left you to scry, something happened, and before any of you jump on me, the waters in the scrying bowl told me to do it." He takes a deep breath as he studies his audience. "It turns out, our memories were taken from us."

I look to Dax, who's listening to Ambrose catch them up on what he saw and how they were all once humans.

"Dax?" I whisper.

"Yeah, Addie?"

"Listen, about the way we left things . . ." His forehead wrinkles and he puts his hand on my arm, nudging me to the side. We take a few paces back against the wall and away from the crowd. "I'm sorry for getting so angry with you. I was just . . . so sick and tired of being lied to."

"No, Addie, I'm the one who is sorry. I still shouldn't have kept anything from you."

I shake my head. "No, Deacon asked you to lie to me so that I wouldn't go off distracting Ambrose. I get it and she was right. I would have. She lied to both me and Ambrose and if she were still here—I'd forgive her too."

Dax cocks his head back. "Wow . . . I don't know where you went to, but something sure as hell happened. The Addie I know isn't so forgiving."

"Hey, that's not true!" I slant my smile and playfully punch him on the shoulder. He chuckles and pulls me in for a hug. I couldn't stay mad at my brother anyway. We fight and then we make up. That's how it's always been.

"I think the best course of action is for each of you to walk into the waters, either one by one or in small groups," Ambrose continues. His frown deepens. "My empathy, that you all shunned before . . ." He searches the room, reading all their expressions, but the reapers haven't stopped to gossip or protest. They're all listening intently. "The waters say it is a power. Why or how I am not aware of yet. But there it is."

His hands drop to his side. "The Judge had a power to take away our memories. Otherwise, I don't know how else he did it. Deacon had developed her power of reading our minds, I don't know why, but by studying the way Dax developed his, and how I developed mine, I can only assume it was because she needed it. So, each of you, before or after, need to develop your power."

I swear you could hear a pin drop in this room. No one says a word; they just stare at him. One of the reapers scratches their head and looks around.

"So, they need to transform their inner selves to reach their higher potential?" My father finally breaks the silence, and my eyes widen. Did he just recite Azazel's words? I snap my gaze to him. "That's alchemy, I can help with that." What the hell? I guess I shouldn't be surprised . . . my powers come from him, don't they?

Ambrose raises his brows and nods rapidly, a smile appearing on his face. "Orlando will help some of you into the waters and talk you through trying to find out who each of you were when alive and what your powers are."

Out of the corner of my eye, I see Evander and Blaise walking to a corner on the opposite end, behind the reapers. I squeeze my brother's shoulders and run over to the shifters.

"Hey . . . uh, Blaise, is it?"

She grimaces at me and holds her hands out in front of her.

"Hi there, Addison," Evander says.

I flick my gaze between them. "I was thinking that maybe I should go with. Seeing as how . . ." I shrug and let a fire ball appear in my hand.

"You're a demon," Blaise finishes, and I quirk a brow at her.

"Yes . . . I might be able to persuade some demons, while collecting prisoners to bring them back to LLAPS." Skadi spots me from where she's trying to get at Crowley and dashes toward me, bumping me in the knee. "Skadi," I growl. "Sit. Behave." Skadi drops to the floor immediately, at my command, and tilts her head.

Evander chafes his chin. "I don't know many people who can command a hellhound. Maybe she does have persuasion over demons." He bumps Blaise in the elbow, and she grunts.

"I agree." She grits her teeth. "Having a demon on our side can be useful." She smiles, although I think it's forced.

I'll take it. No idea why she hates me so much, but it's a start.

Ambrose and Dax walk through the crowd over to us. I hadn't realized he had finished his speech.

"It's settled then. The three of us need to leave ASAP. Addison, Are you ready now?"

"I was born ready." I smile. Blaise rolls her eyes.

"Good. We'll need that attitude out in the field," Evander says.

"Wait, Addison, where are you going?" Ambrose tries to place a hand on my arm and I shimmy away.

"I'm going with them. I can help." And this gives me a perfect excuse to get away from you for a little while. I clear my throat.

"She's got a point," Dax says. "Besides, we had begun to round up prisoners before. But now, I'm sure Addie can manage a lot more than one at a time."

"I think she can be of help," Evander agrees. "Don't some of them think of her as queen?"

"She told the hellhound to sit, and it actually listened. Don't they like . . . never listen to anyone?" Blaise asks.

Ambrose screws his face up. "Yes, the hellhound race was Azazel's. They only listened to him and while he was imprisoned, they ran amok around LLAPS. No one was ever able to control them."

"Till now." I smile, but Ambrose's frown deepens.

"I don't like this, but I know there's no way to talk you out of it." He searches my eyes.

"Nope."

He closes the space between us and lowers his voice, despite the others being in hearing distance. They awkwardly back up and start talking amongst themselves with Dax.

Ambrose's features soften as he looks at me, and my stomach clenches. "You can still be hurt, you know. Lorcan can still kill you."

"I'll be fine. I'm here to save Earth and that is what I intend to do."

"I'll be watching. Stay safe." He'll be watching? Not sure if that's supposed to make me feel safe or creeped out.

"Ambrose . . . I just need some space." I start to back up. "Okay?" I can see the hurt in his face when I say that, but I turn away to face the others.

"Ready?" I ask.

"Let's go kick some demon butt," Blaise says.

Evander opens a white portal with silver swirls and the three of us plus Skadi step through.

LET THE TRAINING BEGIN

AMBROSE

"*How* many reapers are there here?" Orlando mutters under his breath.

"Thirty-three, not counting myself or Dax."

"Okay, how about we put them in three groups of eleven?"

"That's a good idea. The three of us will take separate groups, each group going into a separate Akashic chamber." Okay, that makes it more manageable. I announce the order, and everyone rounds up to separate groups. "My group stays here. Dax, show Orlando where he and his group are going to be, and you go to an adjacent chamber." After about twenty minutes, they disperse.

I stare at my group. Most of them watch me in silence while a few others look confused as to what they think I might do. "Right then, let me have the first group of five." They look among each other, and five reapers step up. "The rest of you, line up in two single-file lines in the back and continue sparring. Now, you five, let's walk closer to the water."

Hesitantly, they exchange glances. "Are you sure this is

right?" Clove says. She was the first one who volunteered to be in my group, so all of her trust in me has been lost.

"Clove, I am asking you to trust me. I walked in and the waters did not become contaminated. In fact, I do not believe that we as reapers carry anything able to contaminate it. Think about that for a second. What are we exactly, if not born from the Akashic? If what I say is true, the Judge took away our burdens, so we have nothing to contaminate the water with." The five of them relax their shoulders but don't say a word. I hold my hand out to her. "Are you ready?" She takes a breath.

"Yes." She takes my hand.

"Oh, you must disrobe first." I pull my hand back. "Perhaps this garment can contaminate the waters, you know, because it's dragged around between this world and that . . ." I chuckle and they laugh. She unfastens her robes and folds them, laying them neatly on the stone. I offer my hand for balance and she takes it, dipping one toe, and then her foot. She winces, as if expecting something terrible to come out of the water and swallow her up for committing such a taboo act. Or as if the previous Judge would come out of the woodworks and reprimand her. Soon, she is shoulder deep in the water and she turns around to look at me.

"Good. Now dunk your head." She gasps but does what I say. A moment later, a yellow light twinkles around her head.

One of the reapers steps up beside me. "What happens now?"

"We wait."

"How long?" I chafe my chin. I'm not sure how long I was under the water, but I wouldn't doubt there was a time-lapse and it just felt longer. Before I could finish my thought, she emerges, gasping for air. And looking fully human. Still dead but shifted to her human form . . . She looks so young, no older than sixteen, seventeen tops. I quickly grab her robes and hold them out to her, shielding my eyes and giving her privacy. Clove grabs them and erupts in nervous laughter.

"I felt the same way when I got out. Tell us, what did you see?"

"I–I . . ." she stutters, searching for the right words. "I was only sixteen . . ."

"Go on . . . " I say gently.

"I think there was a war . . . and my home was bombed."

"I reckon there'd be a lot of casualties of war among us. I too died during a war." I wonder if this is by the Judge's design. I won't know until the rest follow suit.

She looks to the others. "It's true what he says. I was human before this. I wasn't created as a reaper." They drop their jaws and look at each other before rushing to go into the water. I laugh.

"One at a time, you'll all get a chance." The next one disrobes and steps in. Comes out as a guy in his twenties having died a fighter pilot. I'm beginning to see a pattern here.

After him, we had a middle-aged fellow, from times of the Romans, another warrior as well. Teams of five would swap with the newly discovered reapers who went back into training but taking moments to reflect and talk about their experiences in the Akashic. Every so often, I'd flick my gaze to them, expecting them to follow orders and continue sparring, getting ready to take on Lorcan's army. But they wouldn't. They held a new light in their eyes. I mean, can you blame them? They thought they were created to be this robotic force—a unity to collect souls, ask no questions, always follow orders. I've completely shattered their perception of their reality. Each one comes out of the water excited, but then that quickly fades to conflict and confusion. The Judge they followed blindly had lied to us all.

A few hours of this passes and I wonder how Dax and Orlando are doing with their groups. Would the reapers that went with Orlando have followed his orders? They don't even know him. No, they would have because I requested it. I look up and see Clove explaining her human life to another reaper who had also experienced the Akashic memories. I scan the room.

"Those who have not yet been inside the waters, please step forward." Three reapers separate from the crowd and come forward.

"Three? That's it?" They swap glances and nod. Excellent. "Clove? Go to where Dax and Orlando are, ask them how many reapers they have left to go into the water. If they're finished, bring them back."

"Right away."

My last group steps out, and as I had suspected, they were all either soldiers or military personnel of some sort. Some of them did not die in battle, or on the field, or deployed. Some did live on to old age, retired. It's almost as if the Judge was planning a war, or getting ready for one, with capable and experienced people for the job. This was strategically planned. He could have been anticipating Azazel's escape. I cross my arms. Or something else.

But then why take everyone's memory? Was he planning on giving them back? As I'm doing now? No. He wouldn't have done that, I don't think. Maybe he knew we'd develop our powers with some sort of training he had planned for us. It'd be great to know that was true.

Orlando's group walks in first before Dax's. My eyes light up as they come in, cheery yet exhausted.

"How'd it go? I ask.

Orlando chuckles. "You were right. All human." I inch closer to the both of them, bringing them in so that no one would hear. Dax raises a brow.

"Did you notice a trend with how they lived their lives?"

"What?" Dax says. "All soldiers?"

"Yes! Were they?"

He straightens himself. "Every single one."

"Interesting. The question is why."

"Well," Orlando says, "the sooner we can figure that out, the sooner we'll be able to help them develop their powers. I took each of them aside, one at a time after they emerged, to see if they felt any different in that department."

"And?"

"I gave them a simple magickal task to do, to just hold out their hands and bring them in and out to see if they'd form a magnetic field." He holds out his hands in explanation. "You see, no matter what power they develop, magick is energy. They should be able to emanate it through their palms if they have it. But none of them could."

"So, the question is not only how do they develop their powers, but what does having had military affiliations have to do with the power they develop?"

"That's the missing link," Dax says, and I pretend to understand what he's referencing. "If we find out that connection, it'll make our task easier."

"Well, good thing we have two reapers who have developed their powers, then." A glint shines in Orlando's eyes as he crosses his arms.

SAVING MARGARITAVILLE

ADDISON

"How many hours are left before HAPS sends down their army?" Blaise asks as we step out of the portal by a pier on Key West. The cool sea breeze smacks me in the face, bringing me back to a time before this all started. The ocean waves crash, and I can almost hear children playing at the beach . . . Wait, those *are* children playing! What the hell?

Half distracted, I take out the hourglass. The sand has only filled about a tenth of the bottom end of the glass. "That much?" I ask.

She scrunches her lips and turns to Evander, who has already started walking.

"Hey, there are people out there on the beach! The portals really hadn't reached here at all . . . ?"

"No, those portals only opened at the location you were in order for the reapers to find you, I was told," Evander says. Right, that makes sense. So, the portals were confined to only Tavernier, till I took them to Miami. I wonder if it got worse in Miami after I left.

"Now, demons are showing up in municipal areas

among humans," I mutter. This is starting to give me a headache. Cars sit in traffic on Duval Street as people sit outside of coffee shops in shorts and bathing suits, sipping Frappuccinos and going on with their daily lives. Skadi's tail whips my thigh as a pirate dressed from head to toe in full garb walks past us, reaching his shop, Pirate's Treasure Trove. I smile to myself and yank her back. How I wish I could just spend the day here at the beach, watching pirates drink rum while doing pirate shows and selling pirate clothes.

"Blaise, do you have a location?" Evander's tense stature and tall silver and white horns stand out in public. I wonder if anyone will notice us, or if we'll just look like we're dressed up for some sort of ren fair. Can't think of any going on right now, but people down here are often used to seeing people dressed in funny clothes. At least I hope so. Maybe I should have left Skadi back though. She tries to fight my grasp and I realize she's not after the pirate but the direction he was going.

"I'm on it." Blaise looks down to a little circular mechanism in her hand that resembles a compass, but instead of an arrow, it has blinking lights forming a swirling design. The lights blink green a few moments, spiralling clockwise, then change to red and switch to counter clockwise.

"What's that?" I ask.

"This is a *daemrianire*. It's basically a demon tracker." She pauses, turns to her left, and points. "It's pointing this way, come on."

"I could have just let Skadi go for that." Blaise scoffs just as Skadi takes off. We jog after her, heading down Duval Street and making a right turn at a corner, passing a few art shops on the way. No one here seems to have an idea that a literal monster from hell is wreaking havoc on their streets. No one has a clue about how much danger they're in.

Screams erupt from around the corner. Now they do.

"I think we found it." Blaise points to the top of a building. A giant gargoyle-like demon with red streaks of light down its back lurches from over a dress boutique storefront. Across from it, I recognize the type of demon it's fighting. I had seen that type before when Azazel was guiding me down the prisons. It has wings and tendrils where its jaw should be. This was one of the bastards that would take prisoners from the pit and beat them or throw them back into the fire only for them to come out to repeat it all again. Why are they fighting?

People scatter. A car crashes into another and screams engulf the area as the two demons battle it out.

"What do we do?" I shout. Evander and Blaise take out bows and arrows from their quivers.

Blaise shouts through the screams. "Well, we have two options. Kill them, or let them kill everybody else."

I dart my eyes up to the gargoyle-demon. "I doubt one of your little arrows is going to do much to that guy."

"Dragon fire can kill them, remember?" She blows a little smoke, and it catches the tip of the arrow on fire. My breath hitches; Skadi growls. Dragon fire. I had heard of this before.

The only thing that can kill a reaper is the Judge's scythe . . . and dragon fire. Ambrose's words during our fight with the scorpion-demon.

I wish I had paid more attention to my dad's dragon mythology books. Out of the corner of my eyes, a burnt demon drags its flesh across the pavement, unphased by the monsters fighting, or the people running. I need to get that guy back in LLAPS. In fact, these two also belong down in

LLAPS. And one of them is a guard. This is really bothering me. Why are they fighting each other? That guard should be helping to bring the prisoners back. Despite me not liking the bastards, they do serve a purpose.

"Wait!" I yell.

Blaise curls her lips, keeping her arrow centered. "Having second thoughts, demon?"

"If I can figure out why they're fighting, maybe I can stop this. I think Cthulhu-guy over there is just trying to get gargoyle-demon back to LLAPS. I mean, that's his purpose, right?"

"You act like I know your laws. All I know is they're putting humans in danger and they both have to go down."

"What if I can help Cthulhu-guy get the other one back to LLAPS?"

"How? We don't have the time!"

"Just hold your fire; let me try." I have no idea how, but if I can manage to help it, maybe I can persuade Cthulhu-guy to help me get the rest of the escapees. What's better than more manpower? More demon power.

"I'm going to try and help him stop the gargoyle." Just as I say that, the gargoyle grabs a parked car and lifts it directly above Cthulhu-guy. He holds it overhead and drops it. Cthulhu-guy lunges to the right as the car crashes down to the pavement, breaking a parking meter. Pieces of it fly off and fling into a store window. People scream and run. I squint into the car. It looks empty. What would a car insurance claim for a demon accident look like?

I snap my gaze back to Blaise as she pulls her arrow back further, aiming at Cthulhu-guy, while Evander continues to aim at the gargoyle. "We can take them both out right now and save these civilians."

"And then what? Go around Earth killing every demon?

That could take years! Our best chance is to let me persuade as many as I can to *help us!*"

"Demons help us? Now I know you're crazy!" She fires the arrow. I hold my hand up and stop it mid-flight, turning the fire to ice. She widens her eyes and Evander drops his bow.

"Let . . . me . . . try," I insist.

"Fine! What will you have us do?"

I spin the arrow, so the back end is facing Blaise as I hand it over to her. She gives me a side-eye as she takes it from me. "Just watch my six," I tell her.

She pauses, pursing her lips before taking a step back and giving me a nod. "Okay, the plan is to restrain the gargoyle without anyone getting hurt." Debris lands in front of me and I sidestep, shielding myself from getting hit by large pieces of construction.

Eyeing the gargoyle, I consider my options. What powers does the gargoyle have that I can oppose? I raise my palm facing its direction and a circle of fire emerges from the ground, trapping it. A wide grin spreads on my face and I wipe my hands clean. I turn to face the dragon shifters.

"There. See? I did it."

Blaise's eyes widen as she points behind me. I crane my neck and gasp. Aw, shit. The gargoyle spreads out his hands and sucks the flames into the palm of his hand, forming one giant fireball. Uh oh . . .

Cthulhu-guy darts a look at me and gurgles something from his mouth.

"Sorry . . ." I mutter, offering him a shrug. The gargoyle narrows his eyes at me and raises his fireball over his head. Crap.

Evander and Blaise aim their bows, but I hold out my hand. "I got this."

"Yeah, we can see that!" she spits.

Rolling my eyes, I form a water orb in the palm of my hand. Two can play at this game. Gargoyle throws the fire, but he doesn't shoot it at me like I thought he would. Cthulhu-guy flies backward as it shoots at his direction. I throw the water orb directly at the fireball, hitting it right out of the air. Bullseye! I jump, fist-bumping the air. Hot steam dissipates as soon as the elemental balls hit. But of course, the gargoyle is from the pit. Water must be his nemesis then, right?

Cthulhu-guy waves his arms at me and grunts. No idea what he's trying to tell me through his tentacles, but I'm about to save his ass, so move out of the way buddy! I send out a wave of water right to the gargoyle's face, hitting him like a firefighter's hose. I blast him for about a minute. Lowering my hand, I squint my eyes. He hasn't moved. I take a step forward as he stands upright, head bowed and veins popping from his neck and bare shoulders. It didn't phase him. Oh boy.

I turn to the dragons. "What do you think he's doing?"

"I don't know, but it looks like he's recharging . . ."

Recharging? I flick over to Cthulhu-guy, who is now standing, staring at the gargoyle. I snap my eyes back over and . . . Oh, crap . . . Lumps . . . Big lumps of molten lava are appearing on the gargoyle's skin as he grows.

"Now you've done it!"

"Well, how was I supposed to know that would happen?"

"You should have just let us take them out!"

"Look, Cthulhu-guy is on our side, okay? He just wants to . . ."

ROAR

Gargoyle leaps and slams down on the ground, cracking the street open. My knees wobble and Skadi, who had been waiting for my command like a good, trained hellhound, growls beside me. I hold her back with my leg and the gargoyle takes another jump. When he's in the air, I hold my hand out and blast wind to keep him up, strong enough to suspend his wings in flight so that he can't move.

Cthulhu-guy groans at me, nearing where I'm standing. "Yeah, you can help at any time, dude!" I yell, keeping my hand raised. He points at the tree and then to the gargoyle. I quirk a brow. No idea. He bends down to the ground and takes a bit of dirt in his hands and throws it toward the gargoyle. Earth?

The winds start to zap like the sounds of a tornado forming and my jaw drops.

Son of a bitch! "He's using the winds to power himself!"

"Stop the winds!" Blaise yells. I quickly move my hands and the winds settle down. The gargoyle spins himself into a tornado and throws a power surge of air straight at us. My wings immediately spread out of my back and cover my body. I can feel Skadi next to me, holding her ground. When it stops, I stand and notice the shifters have done the same, but Cthulhu-guy got flung above us with his torn, bat-like wings. He hits the side of the building and almost crash lands but catches his balance. He looks at me and grunts.

"Okay! Earth, got it!" The gargoyle works with more than one element. I look at the gargoyle. "Hey, bully! I'll give you something to wrestle with!" I flick my hand over to the ground. Large philodendron vines break the cement, finding their way to the gargoyle's legs and wrapping sharp thorns around him, pulling him down. He jumps up in flight when one touches him, but another vine comes from his right and binds him to the ground. From there, I raise more vines, causing them to circle around him, creating a thorny cage. Soon, he's completely enclosed. He holds onto the thorny vines, wincing, and begins to pull. But with every surge of strength, my vines hold him together, enclosing the space more and keeping him in.

"Gotcha."

My chest heaves and my stomach lets out a loud growl. I'm out of breath and starving. I look back at the shifters, who are putting their bows away. Blaise motions to Cthulhu-guy with her chin. I snap my gaze to him as he walks toward the caged gargoyle. I make my way over as well. People had run and fled during the fight, but since all the ruckus has settled, they're slowly trickling in with their camera phones. How are we going to explain *this*?

My jaw drops when Cthulhu-guy places a hand over Gargoyle's giant hand and gives off a whimper. What the hell? The gargoyle grunts and moves back.

"Look at his eyes," Evander says. I part my lips as I peer closely into the gargoyle's eyes. Oh . . . they're cloudy. He lets out a growl.

"That one's been hypnotized." Blaise acknowledges. I raise both my eyebrows and glance at Cthulhu-guy in case he too has been hypnotized. Nope. His eyes are a normal, solid black. He snaps a glance at me and despite his deep, menacing glare, I sense there to be . . . sentience. The way his hand is placed on the gargoyle . . . the way he didn't make a move to hurt him now that I think of it. He was trying to get him back. But the gargoyle's been under a spell.

"This is definitely Lorcan's doing. He's using the dagger," I say.

"So, now what?" Blaise looks at me and then snaps her gaze to Evander.

"Well, I can break the spell. He might help out, or he may go home."

"Or?"

"Or he might volcano- or tornado-on and kill everybody."

"Great." She notches an arrow. "I'll be ready."

Cthulhu-guy lets out a weary groan.

"Look," I say to him. He straightens himself, acutely aware that I'm talking to him. "I need your help. I'll try my best to break whatever spell your friend is under, but then I need guys to hunt prisoners. Bring them back to LLAPS. Can you help me do that?"

He lets out a sharp grunt and clicks his heels together. "I'll take that as a yes."

I turn to face the gargoyle from between the vines. I touch his hand where the guard was touching him. He grunts and jerks away, but I try again and hold tighter. He stares at me, and I hold his gaze.

"What are you doing?" Blaise says.

"I don't know yet . . ." All I know is, I don't need the dagger anymore to do what it can do. So, maybe I can reverse this. "I, your queen, release you." Maybe I shouldn't have said "your queen" . . . but I thought it would help. The gargoyle jerks back a little, but I hold him still. His eyes start to darken, and the haziness clears out, bringing in those dark black eyes belonging to a demon from LLAPS.

"Welcome back, handsome," I say.

Blaise chuckles. "Know what, you're not half bad." I chuckle and take a step back, releasing the vines and letting him out. Cthulhu-guy groans . . . happily? At least I think it's a happy grunt. Who can tell with this guy? The gargoyle shakes his head and wipes his face. He looks at me and . . . I think that's a smile. I turn to face the shifters.

"And now we have two allies, instead of dead corpses. You're welcome."

"You still made a mess."

I twist my lips and look at the street. Yeah, she's not kidding.

"But . . . it was impressive. Good job," Evander says. I give him a nod. He doesn't say much, but when he does, it's effective. I think I can get along with these two. I turn to Cthulhu-guy.

"Are we still good on what we agreed on?" He and the gargoyle both face me directly, their eyes fierce and bodies rigid. Oh shit, I spoke too soon. "Guys?" The shifters start notching their arrows, but as soon as I think they're about to attack . . . "Wait."

They bend down on one knee and bow their heads. My jaw hits the floor. They stand at the same time, and I stammer.

"No, I'm not really your . . ." I open my palms in explanation. "You see, I just said that to make the spell work . . . giving it more power, you know?"

"Ah ha . . . yeah, I don't think that matters to them now," Blaise says.

Shit, I'm not taking the reins of LLAPS. Oh well, they'll be disappointed when I leave. "Alright well, never mind for now. You two, go prisoner hunting and take them back to LLAPS. Skadi." She barks. "Good girl, stay close, you're going to learn how to hunt as well, without eating them so that I can gather them up and take them home unharmed. And you two . . ." I face the shifters. "Let's get something to eat. I don't know if you know, but I'm pregnant and starving."

"Got it. Let's move." Blaise fastens her quiver and straps it to her back.

My eyes roam the now busy street as police sirens emerge from the corner while people are pointing and shouting. Eyes landing on us. "Uhh . . . guys? What do we do about the people who just witnessed two monsters attacking each other?"

"Don't worry about that," Evander takes out a small device and holds it up. He presses it, and an iridescent lavender light sweeps the surrounding area.

"What the hell was that?"

"It's a *deermadt* device. It wipes the memory of humans. HAPS has been using it on them for years, but it was actually dragon technology, requested by the angels."

"Woah, you guys are like the mythical hippie versions of the *Men in Black.*"

"No idea what that means," Blaise says.

"It's a movie. Hey, what kind of range does that thing have?"

Evander tucks it away. "I can set the range to whatever I want. I only did Key West, but after all this is over, I'll be sweeping Earth in one go."

"And their camera phones?"

"Yeah, none of those pictures will show up, don't worry." Huh. Cool. Maybe we can get things back to the way they were before my mom releases the angels.

We turn to leave when a zipping sound emerges from across the street. My eyes flick up when another zipping echoes through the air. Then another. And another. Portals are opening all around us.

"Crap!" Blaise shouts.

"What is it?"

"Lorcan's army is here."

DEMON-DRAGON CRIME FIGHTING TEAM

ADDISON

We're surrounded. Reapers land in from the sky instead of walking out of the usual vent portals. What's gotten into them?

Cthulhu-guy and the gargoyle who were just about to leave to go hunting for more hypnotized demons stay close instead. It's good to have two demons on our side. I just hope Lorcan doesn't get to them. Reapers and gray-eyed demons circle us. It's like they knew I released one of Lorcan's hypnotized demons. But how?

Skadi takes a step forward and growls. One of the reapers points their scythe to her and lets out a bright red light. "No!" I push Skadi out of the way. She jumps up and bites down on the reaper's skeletal leg. A flash of light erupts from the scythe and sends Skadi flying against one of the shop windows. She lands with a crash and a high-pitched whimper. I spin around and run to her.

"Skadi?" I nudge her a little. She got hit with a scythe blast, for Pete's sake. "Skadi?" She lets out a little growl. She's okay, just hurt. I pat her on her head and stand, facing the reaper. No one hurts my hellhound. I raise my palm and send the reaper an electrical blast of my own. The reaper flies outward. I think I see her bones breaking but then coming back together as she lands.

"Addison!" Evander yells, motioning for me to move out of the way with his hand. "Stand back!" I move my gaze back to the reaper bitch who hurt my Skadi. She snickers at me, but I do what Evander told me to do and take a few steps back, unmoving my gaze.

Evander shifts first. A bright light illuminates around him as he lengthens in size, a large gold and iridescent tail and wings stretching from his pastel white coat. His horns stay the same as the rest of him morphs into dragon form. Blaise follows suit, her shade more of a mother-of-pearl shimmery coat of white, blue, and pink. Outside of LLAPS and under the sun, I can see her fully. My lips part. That was awesome.

They fly overhead. People run in different directions. You'd think they'd learn from the first time to get out of Dodge when the two demons are fighting. But no, they have to come back to take pictures and get themselves stuck in another supernatural fight. Shit. I have to get these people to safety.

"Everyone just move back," I shout to them. Screw that. "Everybody run!" A few people heard me but were already sprinting away. A couple of them get caught in the crossfire. A few feet away from me is a mother and child hiding behind the car that had flipped over, and behind are three reapers of Lorcan's army. I lock eyes with her and stick my thumb out, motioning for her to move to her left, my right. If anything happens, I'll cover them until they get to safety. The woman nods and makes a run for it. A tall, lanky demon intercepts. He has arms stretched down to the floor, with loose skin that drags to his knees. I hold out my palm to blast him when both the gargoyle and Cthulhu-guy fly over. Gargoyle battles the hypnotized demon while Cthulhu-guy takes the woman and escorts her and her child away from the fight. At first, she screams. She darts her eyes back toward me and I nod reassuringly. "It's the only chance you got." Doubt she heard me, but she seemed to understand.

Reapers hold out their scythes to Blaise and Evander. Er . . . I know dragon fire can kill reapers, but can reapers kill dragons? If so, there are only two of them. This isn't a fair fight. They let out a surge of flame and a few reapers jump out of the way, while others disappear inside portals only to reappear a few paces away. Fire hits a few reapers who don't make it into their portals in time.

At first, they freeze, then turn to ash.

My mouth parts as I watch their dust fall to the ground. Just like that. The last time I saw that happen was when the Judge died. Lucifer had the power to kill him the same way. But Lucifer is an angel. Does that mean the angels have the power to—

A blast hits Blaise's side and I snap my gaze to her, interrupting my thoughts. She blocks it with her wing, but it still singes. I can tell she's hurt. Reapers surround them. There's too many of them. I wave my hand and vines start growing from the ground, grabbing onto the reaper's ankles, and holding them in place. More black, thorny vines grow as I confiscate the scythes from their hands. Checkmate, assholes.

A loud zipping sound comes from overhead. One oval-shaped portal emerges above the fight. It stays there, dark and ominous for a few moments.

I flick my gaze over to where the reapers are held in place. Most of them are unmoving, but still staring at the dragons who now stare at the portal. Blaise huffs smoke from her nose and I crane my neck back to the oval hole in the sky.

Lorcan emerges from the black abyss. Rage fills my veins as he floats down to the bottom, leading more demons behind him. I flick my eyes back to the dragons. Evander is already gliding toward Lorcan, breathing fire from his lungs, when Lorcan snaps his gaze and points the dagger—my dagger—to Evander!

The dagger shoots a red glow and Evander sways to the right, hitting the side of the building. Blaise speeds toward him.

"No!" I scream. I have no idea what the dagger can do to dragons, but I do not want to find out! She stops mid-flight and stays in the air, flapping her enormous wings, her eyes staring down at Lorcan. He waves a small pouch in front of her. I don't know what she's doing. Why isn't she moving? I try getting her attention and shake my head. *Not without a plan.*

Lorcan opens the small pouch and tips it into his mouth, swallowing. What the hell is he eating? I squint, trying to make it out. It's my pouch of souls! He's *eating* them? My stomach does a flip. He's eating human souls? *Why?*

He tucks the pouch back to his pocket and Blaise releases a surge of fury. You're dead now, motherfucker! Fire encompasses his body. Reapers below don't move. They just watch as their master gets fried by dragon fire. Except, none of them look phased. At all. Not even the demons. I dart my gaze back to Lorcan. After a minute or two of being roasted, Blaise's flames run out, fumes huffing from her throat. They can run out of fire? Who knew?

Expecting to see Lorcan incinerated, my jaw unhinges and drops back to LLAPS. He's completely unhurt. Did the souls make him stronger? He guffaws and turns his gaze straight to me. I swallow. He tucks one foot in and flies . . . *flies?* Down to where I am. I look both ways and then back to him, taking a step back.

This is my moment. How do I defeat this son of a bitch? Quick Addie, think. When defeating the gargoyle, I had tried all my elemental magick. I need to choose the right thing that he can't easily get out of or manipulate. But he has my dagger. Lorcan's white hair billows in the wind as he nears me, his eyes turn white, his pupils completely gone. I gulp. Blaise closes behind him and puffs another cloud of smoke, followed by a blaze of fire. That was quick. Through the flame, I catch a glimpse of Evander getting up and shifting down. He's okay. That's good.

The fire hits Lorcan, but an ethereal shield blocks him from getting singed, completely. Waves of electricity flow through it.

There's still one element I didn't try with the gargoyle. I doubt any of the four elements will do anything to Lorcan. Spirit, though . . . The fifth element that I had reached to fulfil my potential. The understanding that we are all connected. But that's just an understanding. How can I use it? Somehow, I thought taking Lorcan on myself was a good idea. How was I to know he'd be *eating souls*? And that it would make him powerful! Demons gather around behind him, breaking my vines that hold the reapers in place. I don't have time to fight them right now. My focus remains on Lorcan . . . And his eyes haven't left mine. Here goes nothing.

I hold out my hand, meaning to keep him in place. Meaning to keep him from moving any closer. Maybe I can reach him inside his head. Break the spell he's cast over all the demons. Weaken him from the inside and defeat him that way. I have no idea how or if I can do this, but I have to try. I focus on getting inside his mind. *Let me in.* A wave of white light pushes me out, but I fight back. *Let me in.*

My stomach flutters and I start coughing. Choking. My vision blurs as the white light goes away and Lorcan's grimace comes into view. He's holding his hand out, and even though he isn't touching me, pressure tightens around my neck. Tighter. And tighter. And I cannot breathe. Tears well up in the corners of my eyes from the pressure choking the air from my nose. He takes my dagger out of his belt with his other hand and glints the red ruby for me to see.

"I guess I have you to thank for this. I now have all that I've wanted. Power. And I'm completely undefeated. Thanks to you. But now, I think you can understand why, I have to end you."

Gurgles come out from my mouth. My chest aches and I feel myself turning purple. His ethereal shield is covering us completely. I can no longer see the shifters, or the fire, or the demons and reapers. It's just me and Lorcan.

"You and your unborn demon spawn must die. Or you'll be my undoing. And, well"—he snickers—"I can't have that."

Let me in. I try again. Despite me losing consciousness, despite me not being able to think clearly. I cannot let him kill my child. He guffaws.

"You cannot seep your way into my mind. You're too weak." A white hazy cloud surpasses me, blocking now all signs of life anywhere around me. All I see is white and I begin to fall.

A blast shatters my eardrums. A purple light sweeps my line of sight and I realize that me falling meant only to the ground. I hit the asphalt with my face and take a gasp of air. I struggle to pick myself up from my elbows. Now that the blinding white light has gone, I can see Ambrose standing a few feet in front of me, holding his golden scythe, pointing it directly at Lorcan. My stomach flutters, but this time I don't think it's the baby. I push those feelings aside and climb onto my feet, catching my balance. Blaise runs over to me and holds me steady. I give her an appreciative nod and she pats me on the back.

Lorcan points the dagger at Ambrose. They're at a standstill, the tension of a duel. Two weapons of equal strength. Who will shoot first? No one moves a muscle. A second later, vents sound off from portals splitting the sky and reapers start falling in from LLAPS. My eyes widen as they all look . . . human. Not one of them is in skeletal form. I dart my eyes around, looking for my brother, and then stop when I find him. Instead of wearing his usual reaper robes, he's wearing a leather jacket, jeans, and a pair of cowboy boots. What he used to wear when he was alive.

"Are you seeing this?" I say.

"Yeah, what the hell has happened since we left LLAPS?" Blaise says.

My brother turns himself into fire and starts combatting one of Lorcan's reapers.

"Apparently a hell of a lot!" Pun intended. We watch as my brother shatters the reaper's bones to the ground. It'll probably get back up in a bit, but at least that's one down for now. I don't think he can kill them like Lucifer or the Judge's scythe can. I keep waiting for more of Ambrose's reapers to show their power but none of them have yet. Maybe they haven't developed them.

"I think it's time Evander and I shift again. Another battle is about to break out." I give her some space and watch her shift back into her dragon form. Reapers from what's left of the high council battle Lorcan's army in hand-to-hand combat in the center of Key West. Demons run off to probably collect more human souls, but some stay and fight our reapers. Meanwhile, Lorcan and Ambrose haven't moved.

What are they doing? I inch forward. Ambrose flicks his eyes to me, still holding the scythe to Lorcan. Lorcan takes advantage of Ambrose's loss of focus and shoots power from the dagger, but Ambrose ricochets it in time. The purple and red power interweave and fly off into a tree, electrocuting it right then and there, giving off burgundy flames. My eyes leave the tree as soon as Lorcan opens a portal and disappears into it. My mouth flies open. He just left? I look back to Ambrose and walk toward him.

"Ambrose . . . How did you know?"

"Are you okay?" Dread fills his eyes as he reaches for me.

My stomach somersaults. "Yes, thanks to you. You saved me . . ."

"Of course. I will always save you."

My face reddens and he clears his throat. "We were watching the waters. The reapers have come into their memories but haven't developed their powers yet. We were trying to learn how to do that when this fight came into view in a wave. We immediately assembled and came to your aid."

This is the second time I find myself unable to ever match what Ambrose has done for me. Finding a way for my brother to stay "alive" was the first thing. But now, saving my life and my . . . I place a hand on my stomach . . . baby. A baby I hadn't fully accepted until now. I almost died and all I could think of was that I couldn't let *it* die. My eyes flick up to Ambrose.

"Ambrose . . . I—"

"Don't worry, Addison. I'll get out of your hair. You asked me for space and I'm respecting your wishes." My breath hitches as he turns away. Right. Space. It's the best thing for me right now . . . Right?

Around us, the fight dies down. Blaise runs over to me.

"Holy shit, you kicked ass. You alright?"

"I kicked ass? I almost got myself killed. You kicked ass! What happened? They all left?"

"Yeah, after Lorcan took off, they all followed suit."

Weird. "Why not just stay and create more havoc?"

"I think they're afraid of Ambrose and his mighty scythe," she chuckles.

"Heh . . . yeah." I cringe.

Evander comes running up as Dax and Ambrose and the rest of the reapers circle us.

"Well, that was fun," Dax says.

I shoot him a look. "Nice outfit."

"Thanks."

"Anyone care to explain why you decided to ditch the robes?"

"To be fair," Clove springs up from behind, "I too would like to ditch these robes. Having found out what I have about my past, I kind of want to get rid of everything that reminds me of the past Judge now."

My mouth gapes open. "Is that right?"

"Yeah," Dax says. "We'll explain everything later but for now . . . What's the plan?"

Ambrose looks up to the sky and scratches the stubble on his chin. "You all still need to come into your powers. Lorcan is strong. Stronger than I imagined. Having the dagger is one thing, but there's something different about him."

"Yeah, he's been eating bloody souls!" Blaise says.

"He's been what?"

I nod. "Yes, human souls. He's been eating them, and it has somehow made him invincible."

Dax whistles. "So now what?"

Ambrose stares at his own reflection on the gold blade of his scythe. "All the more reason to get you all trained up. Properly."

"Yes!" Clove shouts, others cheer. Wow, they really have become more human. If someone would have told them in the past that this was progress, they would have all denied it and said how inappropriate it was.

"Boy, if Deacon could see you all now," I say.

Ambrose grimaces and winces.

"Sorry."

"I think we should split up," Evander says. "I can help you get the reapers ready as I know more about the Akashic waters than anyone else here. Blaise and Addison, are you two okay with working with each other in hunting more prisoners and the like?"

Blaise and I exchange glances and nod.

"I think we've proven we can work together. The demon wench isn't all bad, eh?" She places her hand on my shoulder and I look at it. A moment later she takes her hand back, awkwardly. I smirk. "You're not half bad yourself." She chuckles.

I gasp and she retracts further. "Oh shit, Skadi!"

I run to where she had hit the wall earlier. She wags her tail hard on the pavement at the mention of her name. I run down and scratch her ears. "Are you alright?" She moves up, half dragging her body, excited to see me.

"She'll be alright, Addison," Evander calls out. "She got hit hard by the dagger, but at least she wasn't hypnotized."

"Yes," Ambrose says. "Hellhounds can heal fast."

"Oh, good." I hug her and she urges herself up to stand. "She's alright, then."

I glance up at Cthulhu-guy and gargoyle. "You two want to come with us?" They both nod. "Great, it's a team then." Dax and Ambrose exchange glances.

"A lot has happened." I shrug. "But I think I've found a way to make this quicker before the hourglass runs out and HAPS releases their army."

"Right then, Evander, put Key West back together and make sure no human recollects any of what has happened here today. Reapers come with me back to LLAPS, and Addison's team will continue finding prisoners and hypnotized demons. If anything happens, come straight back to us," he orders me. Not sure how I feel about that.

"Good time to leave then," Blaise says. "I just got another alert for a demon sighting. Prisoners will most likely be there as well."

"You got it. Let's roll," I say.

FINDING THE ROOT

AMBROSE

"*I* can't leave your sister alone."

Dax quirks a brow. "Then don't."

"But she told me she needed space."

"Oh . . . She said this *now*? After you saved her?"

"No, before she left, when we were up by the waterfall, talking."

"Ah. Then you need to give her space. Otherwise . . . I wouldn't want to be anywhere near her if she starts to feel suffocated."

". . . She was being suffocated." I turn to stare at him. "If I hadn't gone near her—"

"No, Spock."

"Oh, here we go . . ."

"I mean figuratively. If she starts to feel overwhelmed by you, she's going to get angry and might possibly cause a storm . . . Literally now with her new powers."

My eyes light up. Suffocated can mean being overwhelmed. Got it. "My worry is . . . you saw Lorcan can hurt her. She might be newly powerful but still not as powerful as he is. She still needs the golden scythe to protect her."

"This is true. What do we do? I mean, she's my sister. I don't want her out there, vulnerable to Lorcan."

Evander walks up with Orlando, having already lined up the reapers in groups. "Waiting on your instruction," he says.

"I mean," Dax cuts in, "we'll be watching them closely in the waters. She's not completely alone. Ever."

I nod at that. He's right. I drop my shoulders. "Alright. I think we need to introduce brute force."

"How so?" Evander says.

"Dax, explain to them what you were doing when you learned you could catch fire."

"I was trying to protect the Ashaninka."

"But explain your surroundings. What were you feeling?"

He furrows his brows. "I was . . . afraid for their lives. I wanted to save them. Raiders had set fire to their huts." His eyes light up. "Do you think that's why I was able to create fire? Because fire surrounded me?"

My eyes narrow. But that won't explain why I developed empathy. The last person I saw before I died was that nurse . . . caring for me . . . And the first time I felt empathy as a reaper was when I felt desperate to save a little boy from Abyzou. But I didn't know it was empathy yet. Then when I saved Dax . . . I think it was starting to develop . . . I gasp.

Dax and Evander screw up their faces. "Want to share it with the class?"

I close my mouth. "Sorry. I think partly, yes. Do you remember anything having to do with fire when you were alive, Dax? You didn't die in a fire; this is why I'm confused."

"Oh, I see." He chafes his chin, deep in thought.

"Maybe it's not so simple," Evander suggests.

"How do you mean?"

"The Akashic may grant you what's in your subconscious. Did you like fire when you lived, Dax?"

"Not particularly, I mean, maybe. Kind of."

"Kind of? Did you or not?" I shift my weight to my right leg.

"Well, my favorite superhero was Ghost Rider." He sighs when I don't make a move. "He was a comic book character that would bounty souls and bring them back to hell . . . I can't help but see the similarity. I died in a motorcycle accident . . . and Ghost Rider rode a motorcycle. Well, the second one at least. The first rode a horse."

"Interesting."

"Looks to me like you channelled your childhood superhero then," Evander says.

"I still can't believe that's possible."

I start to pace back and forth. "No, this is good," I say.

Evander hums to himself. "Yes, but it makes it a little complicated. Their powers may not have to do with the way they died, but a passion of theirs. That can take ages to figure out."

"I don't know. Dax developed it when he needed it. I think all we need to do is put them in dire situations where they think they might die."

"Brutal. How are we going to do that?"

I glance at my scythe. "The only way I know."

"So, you're going to threaten them?" Evander says, exchanging a glance with Dax.

"We"—I point to the both of us—"are going to threaten them." I turn to Dax. "You are actually leaving."

Dax arches a sharp brow. "What do you mean?"

"You just reminded me about something important. There are demons out there killing humans to collect their souls. We have Blaise and Addison out there collecting prisoners and demons, but who's out there looking for those souls?"

Dax sucks in a breath. "Shit, you're right. I'm on it!" He turns to leave.

"Get your father's crane bag."

He stops midway and pivots toward me. "Good idea, mind if I do it my way?" A smirk crosses his face.

"What way is that?" Evander asks.

"I think he means the Ghost Rider way," I say. See? I can keep up.

Dax drops his face and narrows his brows, giving me a quizzical look.

"Did I say something wrong?"

"Ambrose . . . I'm no longer a ghost . . ."

I drop my face and he bursts out laughing. "I'm only kidding; you're learning!"

My lips part. "How do you expect me to keep up with you if you're going to keep messing with me? Oh, forget it. Go, collect the souls and bring them back to LLAPS."

"I'll try to save as many as I can if they aren't quite dead yet."

Evander reaches in his pocket and takes out his *deermadt* device. "Here, take this. You might need it."

"Thanks." Dax takes it and jogs to his father.

"Where is he going to get a motorcycle from?"

"He has one, but I'm thinking of making some alterations to it. Some portal-bearing alterations." I smirk. "Are you ready?"

He raises his eyes. "Tell me how."

"Shift."

"What?"

"Now!"

Evander takes a step back. He trembles as he shifts into a

dragon, his sharp talons stretched and pointing at me. Smoke puffs out from his nostrils as he stares, waiting for my next command.

I stammer back a little, undoing the top of my robes, making myself look flushed. "Help! He's turned on us!" I yell. "Just like he killed Deacon!"

The reapers gasp and jump back.

"Don't jump backward! Do something!" I stretch my neck, nudging Evander to go for the reapers.

Evander takes my cue and turns to them, breathing out a shallow amount of fire. I swing my golden scythe and act as if I'm about to attack him. One of the reapers takes her scythe and points it at Evander. Fire blows from his nostrils, circling the reapers and blocking their path. The room rises in temperature and I can feel the poisonous fumes of the dragon fire.

Maybe this wasn't such a great idea. The floor moves below me as I aim to stead my balance.

"Come on! Attack!" I yell. It's difficult to see through the flames, but some of them gape at me as if disbelieving that I'm not doing anything to help them. Can't they see this is an exercise? The reapers back against each other, clutching their scythes yet knowing it can't do anything to save them against a dragon. My chest tightens. They're really stumped on what to do.

Evander roars and shoots fire into the air. It dissipates above us. Okay, clearly I need to step it up or our cover is going to be blown. "Hey! Cockwobble!" I aim the golden scythe and shoot a purple stream of light right past the whiskers on his face. He jumps back, looks at me, and puffs smoke. I bite down a snicker. He'll get me for that later. "Want more?" I point my scythe at him. He flies over to me and yanks my scythe from my hand, nearly lifting me up in the process. I let go and let him take it away. He flies off to the top half of the room, behind the waterfall, where Addison and I had gone to speak.

"Reapers, he's coming back! I don't have my scythe!" Now that I'm weaponless, surely this has got to help. Evander comes back, blazing fire from his nose. The ground catches fire along the edges of the pond. Now the heat has really picked up. Beads of sweat roll down my back. Evander closes in on the trapped reapers, acting like he's about to pick them out one by one. Yes, that's right. Some of them scream, others use their scythes to shoot power at him. I wince. Dragons can still be hurt by us. He covers his face with his wing and turns to look at me.

Uh oh, don't give us away now!

"Hey! Get away from them! Come at me!" He takes a running start and charges. I have no idea where he's intending to go with this, but as he swoops down, the image of Deacon getting accidentally incinerated by Evander's novice mistake makes me regret this whole thing altogether. I wince as he picks me up with his thick white talons and carries me away. He flies us over to the waterfall, near the high archway.

"Uhh ... Evander? What are you doing?"

"I have an idea," he mutters.

"Good. At least one of us does."

"Stay up here and watch. Let them think I've killed you."

"Got it!" I let out a shrill cry and pretend to be inciner-ated. Ducking behind the stonework near the top of the waterfall, I peek through the cracks where the reapers are now screaming. Maybe they have developed some empathy as well. Evander swoops down and targets them. *Come on guys, search deep within.*

A forcefield hits Evander right out of the air. He plummets down to the water, sending a tidal wave of a crash to splash the fire away.

"Yes!" I scream. I run down the spiral staircase to them, their eyes widening and gaping at me.

"What? I don't understand!" Woodrow says.

Orlando, who had been quietly watching from the sidelines, starts laughing. He steps up, clapping his hands, with a frazzled Crowley perched on his head.

"Which one of you did that?" I say.

They move away, leaving Woodrow to stand on his own.

"That was you? A forcefield! That'll come in handy! Can you do it again?"

Evander climbs out of the water soaking wet and back in his human form. I walk over to him and place a hand on his shoulder.

"I'm sorry about that." I laugh. "That was a close one."

"I cannot believe you two were in on it!" Clove steps up, not a single line on her face showing signs of amusement. "That wasn't funny!"

"But it worked," Evander declares. "And . . . I'm sorry I scared you all. It was Ambrose's idea." Her mouth drops open and then closes.

"So there you have it," I say. "The way to develop your powers is through fear and necessity."

They groan and roll their eyes. "This is going to be fun . . ." she says. I chuckle and turn to Woodrow.

"What were you when you were alive?"

"A fighter pilot."

"Interesting choice of power." I rub my hands together and pace back and forth. I glance over at Orlando. "How do you propose we continue? They'll expect a ruse now."

"I was wondering the same thing."

A dark void surfaces the area. Every light in the room darkens.

"What's going on?"

One by one, each light from the sconces flies over to the group. One of the reapers grabs each light in her hands and snuffs them out.

"What's this?" I take a step forward. She gulps, and suddenly all the lights leave her hands and go back to lighting up the room.

"That was interesting. But this was after the ruse . . ."

"I guess I was still hyped up," she says. My eyes light up.

"Maybe adrenaline exercises," Orlando says.

"Simulations," Evander suggests.

I smile darkly. "Okay everyone, intense reaper training starts now."

HYPNOTIC CONTAGION

ADDISON

"So, you and Ambrose, huh?"

"What?" I flick Blaise a glance as we step out of a portal and land on an empty street about twenty miles from Tavernier.

"Well, I mean . . . that's what he said. Or implied when I had to uncuff you. And then you two went to go talk privately . . ." She says the last word an octave higher, letting it linger.

Oh, right. "Umm . . . Yeah, we were a thing once."

"Once? Why did you guys break up?"

I screw up my face. Because I had sex with a demon overlord when I thought it was Ambrose and now I can't bear to look him in the face without seeing horns grow from his head. And there's the whole APB thing. So much for me keeping my mind off it.

"Look, sorry I asked. I don't mean to pry . . . it's just . . ."

"What?"

"It looks like you two aren't over each other, that's all." That's because we aren't.

"It's kind of complicated." I spread my hands out. "I care

a lot about him, but . . . I'm pregnant with someone else's kid and . . ."

"Oh . . ."

"No, I mean . . . it's not like that. I was deceived." Horribly deceived. I explain the details to her, and she gets quiet while we walk side by side along a boardwalk to our next demon sighting.

"That's tough. But . . ."

I flinch. "But?"

"I don't know. . . You said it yourself, he doesn't fault you and even said he'd help raise the child. I don't know about you, but where I come from, a man like that is hard to find."

I swallow and smile.

"If you two care about each other still . . . Don't let all that get in the way."

"So, how about you?" I say, changing the subject.

"How about me what?"

"Any dragon shifter you're into? What's up with you and—"

"No!" She laughs. "Evander is my cousin."

"Oh, my bad. I didn't know." The resemblance makes sense now. Both of them in dragon form have a white coat and shimmery, pretty colors.

"That's okay . . . but while we're on the subject . . ." Blaise moves her eyes down to the sidewalk.

"Hm?"

"So, Dax is your brother?"

My brows hit the top of my forehead. She has a thing for my brother? Yuck. But okay, I did see them sneak glances at one another during Ambrose's speech. Huh. "Yeah, he is."

"And he's a reaper . . . Wow."

"Yeah, he um . . . died in a motorcycle accident a few

years ago. A lot has happened since then, but thanks to Ambrose, I get to have my brother back."

Cthulhu-guy and Gargoyle take off flying. Blaise looks down at her device, the reflection of the sun shining off it.

"What's going on?"

"We're walking into prisoner territory but . . . there are demons on the loose. I just can't tell where."

"You can't tell where?"

"Not yet."

That's weird. I squat down next to Skadi. "Okay Skadi." She licks my face. "No! Bad girl!" Yuck. I spit. "Skadi, hold still. Listen to me." I point my finger and create an egregore on the palm of my right hand. "Here, eat this." She gulps it down, leaving my hand full of hellhound saliva. I wipe it on my pants. Gross. "There's more where that came from. Do you want more?" She whimpers. "You have to go find souls, but don't eat them! Bring them back, and I'll give you more!"

Skadi barks twice.

"Is she going to listen?"

I shrug. "Sometimes she does." Here's hoping. I create another egregore and toss it to her. "Good girl, now go!" She kicks up dirt as she runs into the street. With those three doing their job, or at least two that I know are doing their job, hopefully we can bring back a large number of prisoners.

Moans come from the street. Uh oh. Blaise and I look at each other and make a sprint toward the sound. We race down the street and make a right turn at the corner street lights. No one is around watching, and no cars are moving around this area. That moan reminds me of . . . shit.

A zombie turns the corner. In an instant, Skadi tackles it to the ground. Not exactly what I told her to do, but honestly? What else do we do with these zombies? They don't have a spirit. We can't just let them roam around, and there's no saving them.

"Addison, look!"

I follow to where Blaise is pointing. Burnt ones and tortured souls from the prisons revolt in the street. Demons with milky eyes taunt them, trying to get them to either become food for Lorcan, or become one of them.

"We have to separate them!" she says, just as she gives off a subtle tremble and shifts back into her dragon form. I won't ever get used to that.

"Don't hurt them!" I yell. I watch as she flies over to the fight between demons and prisoners and bulldozes her way between them. Cthulhu-guy and Gargoyle try to take the prisoners from the sidelines who are not in direct contact with the demons, but the prisoners are refusing. I mean, why would they want to go back to LLAPS? I don't blame them. After all this is over, I do have to implement a plan to make things better down there. I mean, before I go back to living my life.

I sprint over to where they're wrestling with some prisoners.

"Hey!" I call out. One of the prisoners pushes me to the side, and I nearly topple over but catch myself against a brick wall. I turn my neck to see a burnt one meandering around and I make a dash for him. He sees me running, squeals, and makes a run for it. Oh no, you don't!

Last time I met these guys I was grossed out and afraid, now I'm chasing one of them! What would interest one of these guys? Besides not being burnt flesh for eternity? "Hey . . . I can offer you your freedom," I say. The burnt one stops and turns to me. Hell yeah, that worked. Now, can I really offer them their freedom? I don't even have a plan put in place yet. The burnt one gapes up at me and I squat down.

"Come with me, and I promise you I will try and make things better for you." His flesh droops over the side of his face as he stares at me in silence. Cthulhu-guy spots us and comes over. The burnt one widens his eyes, backing up.

"No, it's okay." Oh shit, that's right . . . This guy was one of the ones who used to torture the burnt ones from the pit. Cthulhu-guy squats down and offers his hand. The burnt one looks at it.

"See? I helped him. He knows things are going to be different. But you need to go back. You don't belong on Earth, okay?" He hesitates but then takes a step forward. I'm going to take that as a yes. I open a portal to a secure pocket dimension for prisoners only, since Ambrose gave me clearance to do so, and let the burnt one in. Someone on the other side is manning all the prisoners that I send in.

"Thanks," I say to Cthulhu-guy, who is taking off to collect more prisoners. At this rate, we'll take forever.

Over to where Blaise is pushing the demons off the prisoners, she tries her hardest not to kill them. I can tell because smoke is huffing out of her nostrils. I run over as more and more demons keep piling on top of her and let the others handle the prisoners for now.

As I reach over to help her, the prisoners pushing into the demons topple over, sending Blaise jumping above them and out of the way, causing her to half shift to catch herself from falling. Her wings catch air and shift back to her arms as she lands over by me.

I twist my face in confusion. "They disappeared?"

"Invisibility. That's why I hadn't seen them on my device."

"Demons that can turn invisible?" I gape. Because, why not?

She snaps her neck to me. "How do you not know your own kind?"

"How many times do I have to tell you, I wasn't always a demon! This is new to me!"

"Right, sorry. I keep forgetting. I guess this is our chance to take the prisoners. We can't do anything about the demons if we can't see them. For now, anyway."

I squint my eyes over to where they were. Outlines of figures catch my eye. I can't see them fully, but . . . I can make out where they are. "I can sort of see them . . . Try to handle the prisoners, and I'll handle the demons this time."

"Deal."

Without the demons visible to see, the prisoners are left dispersing themselves, thinking they've been left alone. A demon zaps himself from behind one of them and grabs them. I stride over, hold my hand out to the prisoner, and take him by the arm, pulling him to me. The demon jerks back, partially making himself visible, showing its orange horns and then disappearing again. I have two targets to get. One to send to the prisoner holding dimension, and another to unhypnotize, and hopefully that'll be enough to get him on my side. Like I did with the gargoyle.

This is going to be brutal. I hold my hand out, the tips of my fingers becoming icy as I start to send ice onto the demon, freezing him in place, but more importantly, allowing us all to see him. The prisoner struggles in his grasp, but the demon flexes his muscles and breaks my ice. He quickly turns to the prisoner and stares into her eyes. The prisoner kicks and squirms. I try to hold on, but I'm flung back by the demon's powerful force. I hit the pavement hard on my back, but I scurry back up, holding onto my stomach. I don't know why I do it; it's becoming a habit.

"Hey, ass hat!" I yell at him. "Let that prisoner go!" The prisoner loosens herself out of the demon's grasp but when she turns to me . . . her eyes are whitened out. Wait—how? I thought only Lorcan could do that! The demon lets out a laugh and the prisoner follows him. "Come back here! Your queen orders you!" Cheap shot, I know, but I needed to try something.

"Blaise . . . !" I spin around to find her. "The hypnosis . . . it's contagious!"

"Yeah! Just noticed that over here . . ."

What does she mean—I run over to her. "Blaise?" She points behind me and I spin around. The gargoyle who I had previously unhypnotized now hovers over us, with his eyes fully white, and beside him is Cthulhu-guy, his eyes also whitened out.

"How . . . the . . . hell . . . ?"

'I don't know, but we have two options. Either get out of here or let me catch them all on fire!"

"You can't just go around catching everyone on fire, Blaise!"

"Not everyone! Just scum and demons!"

"Hey! Look who you're calling scum!"

"I said scum and demons. I'm not implying that you're scum!"

"Well, I'm a demon! Are you going to kill me too?"

"You're different!"

My face reddens. But my kid isn't. "Fine. Now's not the time to fight."

"No, it isn't," she says, and I ball my fist. "Is there any way you can . . . you know, do that thing you did before with this gargoyle, but in bulk?"

I shake my head. "No, I'd need to reach each one individually. Okay, let me think . . . The hypnosis is contagious, and the demons can transmit it to the prisoners. They then attack humans, steal their souls, and leave their bodies to rot as zombies . . ."

"Addison . . . He's backing away . . ."

I snap my gaze up. Shit. We lost two demons that could help.

"Are they leaving?" she asks.

"It appears so. Maybe they know they can't hypnotize us, so they're focusing their energy elsewhere . . ."

"That would mean they can make decisions. I don't think that's it. They're . . . being called back," she says. That makes more sense.

"Why would Lorcan be retreating? What is he planning?"

Skadi barks as she jumps happily, eating hypnotized prisoner after prisoner. "No! Skadi, get back here!"

"Nice to know she listened!"

I shoot her an angry look. "She'll get there . . ." The prisoners disappear with the hypnotized invisible demons and not a minute later, we're standing on a barren street and down the two demons that were helping us. I let out a winded sigh. "Well, that was a waste of time."

"Maybe not . . . We found out that the hypnosis is contagious. What we can do with that, I don't know. But at least it's more information."

I swallow. Can it be passed onto me? No, Lorcan would have taken that opportunity instead of trying to kill me. Unless just killing me was worth more to him. But I'm sure it's because I'm too powerful. "Blaise, do you think you can catch the hypnosis spell?"

She shakes her head. "Dragons can't fall under a demon's influence." That's good news, at least.

The sea breeze brushes through my hair as I stare off into the empty street headed toward the docks. What a mess. There has to be a way to lure all these demons and prisoners into one consolidated spot and unhypnotize them all at once.

"How much longer do we have until HAPS releases their army?"

I take out the hourglass from my pocket. Holy crap. How many hours have passed since I last looked at this thing? Holding it up, I say, "The sand is halfway down. We're running low on time."

"Hopefully the reapers have come into their powers already. Sidhe really needs help against HAPS. I think the only reason they haven't made it down here is because they knew the demons were invading Sidhe first, for the siege over the waters."

"No, that's impossible. My mother wouldn't have planned it that way. I begged her to let me fix things first."

Blaise's eyes turn fierce as she stares at me. "Wait, your mother?"

I gulp. Have I said too much?

"Your mother is an angel?" she stammers.

"Yes, I recently found this out."

"And you begged her? Is she a general?"

"Uhh . . ."

"You have to get her to stop! That's my home they're raiding!"

"Look, I don't know what's going on in your home, but I'm sure my mother has nothing to do with raiding or pillaging anyone."

"Yeah, that's a fresh lie coming from a demon." And we're back to this. Great.

"Blaise . . ."

"Let's just get back to LLAPS. Let Ambrose know what just happened."

I slap my arms against my legs. "Fine, let's go."

THIS MIGHT GET AWKWARD

ADDISON

Blaise knocks on the door to the private training room Ambrose is in with the rest of the reapers. After a moment of no one answering, she pushes it open and I follow her in.

"No! Don't open the—"

A tidal wave of water hits me hard in the face. My wings shoot out, shielding me as I'm soaked from head to toe. The water settles around me. I shake my wings and walk inside.

"Sorry . . ." Blaise mutters, dripping wet.

"Was that Akashic water?" I ask, squeezing my hair dry.

"No, one of our reapers is water powered. We had her suspending the water above our heads but every time she's interrupted, it soaks us all."

My eyes beam. "Wow, so you guys are making progress!"

"Barely," a girl mutters from inside her hood. I walk over to her.

"Hey, the fact that you can create water and control it at will is amazing! Especially since you've just now come into these powers. It took me ages to learn!" Her eyes light up.

"Really?"

"Really. You're doing great."

"Don't worry, you'll get the hang of it," Ambrose says, coming near her. He puts his hand on her shoulder. "Would you like to take a break? Maybe give someone else a try?" My eyes flick to hers as she lowers her eyes and shrugs. Is she blushing? Heat courses through my blood.

"We have some news," Blaise breaks my concentration and I shake it off. We're not together anymore. It's fine. Ambrose looks up at Blaise and Evander comes to join us.

"The rest of you, keep practicing with Orlando." Ambrose walks over to the side of the wall and the rest of us follow.

"What happened when you were on Earth?"

"The hypnosis is apparently contagious," Blaise starts.

Evander folds his arms. "This is new." He sticks out a foot and leans to his left while looking at her.

"Is it?" I ask. "I mean, how much does everyone know about Lorcan's hypnosis spell over the demons? Besides that, it makes their eyes turn white and do as he says."

Ambrose shakes his head. "Before he was collecting demons, and spreading it. If it's contagious, then he's figured out a way to make it spread faster."

"Great, that means more terrain to cover too."

"Not if we get to him first," Ambrose says. True.

Evander sticks his hand out to me. "You were able to break that one gargoyle's hypnosis, though, weren't you?"

"Yeah, but then we lost him and his friend who was helping us."

"Ohhh . . ."

"Yup, they've both been hypnotized." Blaise tightens her lips.

"That's right, very good . . . Now, hold it there!" I turn my head to see my father helping one of the reapers levitate another reaper. A smile curls on my face. Who knew he'd find his purpose in LLAPS?

"Addie?" My attention snaps back to Ambrose.

"Hmm?"

"Did you notice anything else about them? Other than being hypnotized? Anything that could help us figure out how to break the spell permanently?"

I shake my head. "I've been playing it over in my head. From reaper to demon to prisoner . . ."

Blaise cuts in. "The second that demon realized that you were on their side and wanting to help, they both bowed down to you. It still has to do with you."

"Yes, but I can only unhypnotize one at a time. By the time I finish with one and turn to the next, another demon is rehypnotizing the last one!" I sigh. "Not to mention, as you saw, it doesn't last. To be honest, Lorcan's hypnotic power is coming from my dagger . . . The only thing that can truly counteract it is . . ."

"My scythe."

I slant my smile and nod. "Precisely. If only I could amplify my magick somehow and reach more at once."

Evander hums to himself, scratching the top of his head beside one of his horns. I flick my gaze to him as he squints down at the ground. "Ambrose? In our legends, Azazel could send off power from the scythe by him slamming it on the ground. I seem to remember the elders saying it would sweep the land, emanating power from all over."

"That's right."

"Since Addison can control the dagger, and Azazel made the dagger, do you think it could transmit Addison's power, giving her more range?" Ambrose squints at him then widens his eyes. I'm still trying to make sense of what he's suggesting. Amplify my power with the scythe's help? "Furthermore, wouldn't you be able to make the change permanent?"

"Alright, new plan of action." The shifters perk up and my stomach flutters. Something about Ambrose taking charge like this sends a tingling feeling down my core. What can I say? I like a man who knows how to take command. Ugh. I should not be thinking like this right now. Time and place, Addie!

"What do you have in mind?" Evander asks.

"If we can dismantle Lorcan's army, being the reapers, we can isolate the situation by only having to deal with him."

Evander nods once. "I think that's better than trying to do everything at once. At least your reapers are stronger now. The others won't be able to stand a chance."

"You're all forgetting one teeny, little problem," Blaise says. "We still have HAPS to deal with. Right now, we're down here while our people are fighting them for the waters in Sidhe." She gives me a dirty look and I roll my eyes. "Not to mention, HAPS coming down here is also a ticking time bomb."

"She's right."

"How much time do we have on that, Addie?" Ambrose's voice is kind when he talks to me, different from when he makes a command. I check the little hourglass my mother gave me.

"Not much time left, we're running out of sand."

"Great. I have an idea," Blaise says. "Since Addie's mother is one of their generals, how 'bout she goes up and stops her mother from raiding our water?" I let out a loud sigh.

"We've been over this. My mother is not killing any dragons!"

"You don't know that!"

"I think I know my own mother!"

"Enough!" Ambrose shouts. Oh, shit. Is it bad I got turned on a little? He clears his throat. "We haven't received word that's what's happening in Sidhe. No one so far has died, so Blaise, you can relax."

"I believe they're negotiating," Evander adds.

"See?" I spit.

She rolls her eyes. "Fine. But it's only a matter of time before that blows up too. We still need to stop Lorcan before it's too late."

"As I was saying," Ambrose starts, "Addie, I think Evander might be on to something. You and I should unite magick on the hypnotized demons."

"And newly hypnotized prisoners." I gulp.

Ambrose nods.

Crap, this means we're teaming up. On Earth. So much for space. And with my mind going all nuts around him right now. This doesn't leave me time to think.

I open my mouth to protest but then shut it.

"That's probably a good idea," Evander says. "Should we all go up? Bring the reapers?"

Ambrose narrows his eyes as he looks to the reapers in training.

"Hey, where's Dax?" Blaise says, and I smirk. Of course she notices my brother's gone before I do.

"I needed someone collecting new souls while the others train, and since Dax is already experienced with *his* power, I had him go." That makes sense. "But now I'm thinking I need more reapers collecting souls. I think I'm going to split these up. Some of them are doing well enough to go on their own now. Though I'll have to call them back to fight Lorcan."

"He still can't ambush us here, right?" I say.

"No, the portals are still guarded."

"Not by dragons, though." Blaise adds. "Most of us have left back to Sidhe while they and HAPS *negotiate*." She adds emphasis on that last word and flicks a look to Evander.

"That's a good point. We could use more of you guys," he tells them.

"We'll stay and take turns manning the portals and helping Orlando train the reapers." A light reflects off of Evander's horns as one of the reapers behind him shoots out electricity from their fingers. Crowley flies off to hide behind the waterfall and Skadi takes it as an invite to chase him.

"Right then, I'll have the reapers who are ready continue reaping and looking for lost souls." Ambrose turns to me. "And if it's alright with you, that leaves us to go back to Earth and handle this hypnotized army."

I swallow. "Okay."

DEMON FIGHTS AND A JAR OF PEANUT BUTTER

ADDISON

"Why does it have to be Florida?"

"It's where it started, because of you actually."

I sigh. "I know, but it's always Florida. Can't these demons go somewhere a bit cooler?" Ever since Ambrose closed all the portals, the Florida heat has been going back to its normal state of hell. I retie my braid that has gotten messy from all the running around. My stomach roars.

"What was that?" he asks, peering into me.

My cheeks burn. "Sorry, I haven't had a chance to grab a bite to eat. Pregnant lady over here . . ." We step onto a barren street near Key Largo, about six miles away from the house. I scan the area. "Looks like there hasn't been anyone around in a while. Do you think we're too late?" I search the road for zombies.

"No, there is a demon lurking around here. And where there might be demons, there will be prisoners; those are their main targets."

"That's true. Prisoners and people. I guess follow the prisoners and they might hit two birds with one stone." The moment I say that I turn to look at him, expecting to see his face twisted and confused. "Sorry . . . somehow I always do that around you. When I'm around other people, I don't use half as many idioms."

He chuckles. "No, it's alright. I'm getting used to them. Use them, please. I'd like to learn more."

"Oh yeah?"

"Yeah, today I learned about your brother being a ghost rider . . ."

I blurt out laughing. "Now, that's a sight I'd like to see. My brother did love Ghost Rider growing up. He loved comic books in general."

"I heard." He stares down at his scythe as if waiting for it to do something.

"Why did it bring us here instead of somewhere there might be a big sighting?" I ask.

He shrugs. "It could be that there was and they're just hiding out in their own pocket dimension. Just because I closed the portals to LLAPS doesn't mean they still can't hide out in the ether."

"Oh . . ." I hadn't thought of that. But I guess it makes sense that since we still have pocket dimensions, we can go to them without going into LLAPS . . . or HAPS for that matter.

"Why don't we grab you a bite to eat while we wait? There's no reason leaving for another sighting if the scythe is still intent on us waiting here." My stomach grumbles at the mention of that.

"I'm game." He quirks a brow. *Damnit, Addie.* "Yes, I mean yes!"

I search our surroundings. The only place close enough is an empty bar. Damnit, I wish we had landed somewhere closer to a CVS or a Publix. We stride over to *Boozy Penguins* and walk in. "Well, this is at least a pub, so there might be food." Ambrose tries for the door and it swings open.

"After you," he says. I glance at him and walk inside. Lights from the gaming machines are still on and empty stools and chairs by the bar and tables look like no one's sat in them for weeks. I wonder if the food is going to be any good. The floor creaks as I step further in. A few moments pass and I'm still staring at the bar.

The quiet ghost town vibes I'm getting from this place suddenly make me insanely self-conscious about being alone with Ambrose. I turn my cheek slightly and catch him staring at me. I feel my cheeks growing pink and I think of something to say.

"It's strange that more people haven't noticed the apocalypse in nearby cities."

"I had all roads blocked from cities that haven't been affected. My main goal was to isolate cases, chase rogues, and keep the humans from knowing what's going on in the supernatural world." Wow, he acts fast.

"Good job."

"Thanks."

"No, I mean it." I glance at him while walking behind the bar. "You've done much better with this whole "taking charge" thing than I have."

"I think you're doing fine, Addie . . . given the . . ." he pauses, and I can feel what he's thinking. "Circumstances."

"Yeah."

"Um, I'll check their kitchen," he says. "Stay away from the alcohol."

"I wasn't going to drink any—" I stop when I notice the smirk on his face as he disappears. He chooses now to have a sense of humor? Oh, where do they keep their peanuts? I rummage through their cabinets, shifting glasses, a book on bartending and mixology, someone's purse, no peanuts. I open another cabinet and move some full bottles of daiquiri mixes, and bingo! A full jar of peanuts! And pretzels! Yes! "Jackpot!"

Ambrose opens the door with a jar of pickles and a jar of peanut butter in hand! Heaven! "Is this good?"

My eyes widen and I nod happily. "Hell yes," I say with a mouth full of pretzels. "Oh my god, I feel like I haven't eaten in days!" Heavy footprints inch closer to where we're standing and I duck. Ambrose eyes me and squats down too. He presses a finger to his lips and I beckon for him to come closer.

"It's a demon," he whispers. "He's outside the bar. Must be the one my scythe picked up."

"How come we didn't see it a second ago?"

"Probably one of the invisible ones."

I stick another handful of peanuts in my mouth as I nod. Can you blame me? I'm starving and I might not get another chance. "Mmm . . . Yeah, Blaise and I ran into those earlier. Sneaky bastards." I wipe my hands on my pants. "Ready when you are. Let's take this motherfucker down."

"It's best if we let him in here and sneak up on him instead. If we go out there, he'll just disappear again."

Good point. "So how are we going to do this?"

"Just be still, let him come in. He smells us. When he comes to this side of the bar, I'll stun him with the scythe, and together we'll unhypnotize him." I nod. Hopefully, the scythe makes it a more permanent fix and gets him on our side. Minutes pass and the demon is still roaming outside. He opens the door and Ambrose presses closer to me. Luckily, I was able to eat some more pretzels, peanuts, and managed a whole pickle. I'll be good for another twenty minutes.

I become acutely aware of his breath tickling my skin. This is a real tight spot. I sit facing him on my knees while I dip my finger into the peanut butter jar for a taste.

"Addie . . ." he begins. "Since we're alone, I just want to tell you that I truly am sorry . . ." His eyes drop to the floor. "For not having gone after you when you needed me the most."

I swallow and look deep into his crystal blue eyes, wrinkles creasing his crow's feet. I wish I could tell him I forgive him, and that I understand he had a job to do. But . . . I mean, I left Earth to go find him in hell. He couldn't tell Deacon to buzz off and let me know he was okay? To help me deal with becoming . . . This thing? How do I know he'll always be there for me in the future? I ignore his apology and instead answer with, "Thank you for saving me yesterday."

"Of course, I'll never let you out of my sight again."

"It's not about you letting me out of your sight." I need my privacy, come on. "It's about you being there for me when I need you the most." I twist the lid shut on the peanut butter jar and set it down. "I went to LLAPS to go save you because I thought you'd do the same for me . . ." I let that linger.

He swallows and lets out a sigh. "I know . . . I guess, I just wanted to say I'm sorry . . . again."

I flick my eyes back down to the peanut butter jar in my hand. "So . . . I didn't tell you about this before because, one, I've been kinda busy and two . . . I'm still thinking about it . . ." His forehead creases. "My mother gave me a potion that'll turn me human again. And the baby."

"Oh. Huh."

I shrug.

"Is that what you want?"

"Honestly? I don't know. I mean, I'm one hundred percent fine with being a demon now, maybe not having the responsibility of a command but, I like my powers."

"Yet?"

"On the other hand, I have to consider what's right for my baby. LLAPS is a scary place full of devious monsters. I mean, look at how Azazel turned out."

"That wasn't entirely LLAPS' fault, but I see your point. It's a dangerous place. The last thing we want is the baby getting lost in the mental plane." My eyes widen. Or flown away by a gargoyle.

"And you want the baby to live a normal life." He smiles at me and I offer him a sideways smile back, dipping my finger in the peanut butter again and eating it. "Whatever you decide, I fully support you." My heart warms. He places his hand on mine and then pauses; his face grows serious.

The demon swings the door open, breaking it off its hinges. Ambrose holds his finger to his mouth. We don't want it to leave when it sees us; we need to trap him. I take the peanut butter jar and flick it to the floor.

Ambrose looks. I shrug.

"I'm trying to get it to come," I whisper. He opens his eyes, understanding. The demon sniffs the air as it tosses some chairs and tables to the side. I hold my breath, readying myself to use my magick. Ambrose quietly grips the hilt of his scythe and lifts it off the ground, getting himself ready for action. Half expecting the demon to come from the entryway of the bar, I scream as it leaps over the bar, landing on top of me. Ambrose takes his scythe and stuns him in place. I scramble out from under the demon's thick coat and muscles. It has a large wolf-like jaw, and a lump on his back. He almost looks like an old comic book–style werewolf, except only, it isn't a shifter. It's an invisibility demon. Which means keeping it still is in our best interest so that it doesn't disappear on us.

"Addie, now!"

Facing the demon, I place my hand on its head. His eyes, a milky white, ogle back at me. I close my eyes and reach his consciousness, trying to find him. The real him. I search eons of tangled memories. It's like clearing cobwebs inside of an endless void or tunnel. Then I see him. By himself in a puddle of filthy water. It reminds me of where I had gotten lost the first time I met a guardsman. He startles as I approach him. *It's okay,* I whisper in my mind. I take his hand, surprised that he so readily gave it to me. I don't think he knows what's real and what isn't right now. And I pull him back.

I open my eyes and lift his chin. Ambrose still has him held in place. His eyes go from milky white to black. He jerks but can't move.

"He's back."

"Excellent! Good work!"

"Don't release him yet, though. You still need to make that permanent."

Ambrose touches a few dials in his scythe. Hmm . . . I wonder how that works.

"That should do it . . ." He let that linger.

"But?"

"But . . . There's no way to test it. I told the scythe what to do, and that usually does the trick."

I place a hand on his shoulder. "Trust it then, Ambrose. This is the dagger's counterpart. It has to work." I face the demon. "I want to let you go now, but I need your help. Do you promise not to run?" The werewolf-demon nods.

"Good." Ambrose lowers his scythe and releases the

demon, who is now stretching his jaw and neck. "Did you see who did this to you?"

"Lorcan," he hisses.

"Good. I brought you back, and Ambrose made it so that you cannot be rehypnotized. Do we have your allegiance to help us stop him? So that we can fix LLAPS? Fix . . . your home . . ." I added that last part to help him see the bigger picture. Who knows if he caught that?

He takes a step back and bows down, bending a knee.

"What will you have me do, Your Majesty?"

My cheeks flush. This is the third demon to bow down to me, but the first one in front of Ambrose. "Please, get up." I motion for him to stand with my fingers. "That's not necessary."

"Help collect the prisoners and bring them back to LLAPS," Ambrose says.

"Um . . . How will he collect them? The portals are being guarded and he's not a guard who can round them up . . ." Like Cthulhu-guy. Poor dude.

"We're going to need more crane bags."

I take the one I have around my belt loop. I left Skadi at LLAPS so that I wouldn't have to manage her, but I no longer need it to hold egregores for her since I can create them from my fingertips with ease. And I can just open a portal to the pocket dimension. "Here, take this. Collect only the prisoners who aren't hypnotized yet." I hand him the crane bag.

"Give us a day or so, and we'll come back for you to take the prisoners you've collected to a temporary prison."

The demon holds the pouch tight. "Thank you. You won't be disappointed, Your Majesty."

I cringe. "Go now."

We watch as he leaves and I take a few pretzels and dip them in peanut butter. "For the road."

He takes one from my hand and sticks it in his mouth. "This is becoming the new normal for you, isn't it?"

"What do you mean?" I say, chewing.

"You're very casual about dealing with demons now, is all."

I snort. "Why, because I can't wait to eat another pretzel while unhypnotizing a demon? Yeah, I guess becoming a pregnant demon will do that to you." The moment I say that, his demeanor drops.

"I'm sorry ..." he says again.

"I don't blame you for that, you know ..." He lets his silence linger. "So, we're going to have to figure out a way to speed this up. How can we use your scythe to add range to my unhypnotizing technique like Evander suggested?"

"I've been thinking about this too ... How do you do it, exactly?"

"The first time I did it wasn't so intense. I was able to bring the gargoyle back by feeling his presence in his mind. But with this one, I had to search for him inside the depths of his memories, where he was being kept away ..."

Ambrose chafes his chin. "Right, we won't be able to do that for everyone individually ... There's no way ..."

"How about some sort of rope spell?"

"What? And hope they see it and latch on?"

I shrug. He's right, they might not figure it out.

"Actually, you might be onto something there ..."

"How?"

"What if we can imbue it with a note, or a spell that makes them want to grab onto it?"

My eyes light up. "Yes! Like a servatoir! An egregore with

a purpose! I can design it so it morphs into what they want to see in their mind. Something they would follow out."

"And then once they come out of it, the scythe will make it permanent, instantly." My grin widens and I stare at his face. With the scythe's range, I'm feeling more confident we can get this done. His eyes lock with mine and then fall to my lips, awakening a swarm of butterflies in my stomach. My eyes fall to his lips too . . . but I force them back to his eyes.

I missed the way he gets awkward when not knowing what to say, or the way his hair falls over his eyes. Unspoken words fall between us, and I get the biggest urge to kiss those full lips of his. I want to, but I won't . . . I move a step closer . . . But why not? Suddenly, I'm not feeling so set in my decision for space anymore. What's the worst that could happen? I resent him forever?

"We make a good team, Addie," he finally says, and I stop.

My breath hitches. "Yes, we do . . ."

"We need each other . . ." he says. My face reddens. "I mean, for the mission," he amends.

"Y–yes, of course." I clear my throat. "Well, we should get going . . ." I'm not thinking clearly. He grips his scythe and turns halfway toward the bar opening, reaching to take my hand but stopping. I reach out and take his. I can't help it, I want to touch him. It's only his hand.

A deafening crash shakes my bones. Ambrose turns and grabs me as the ground quakes and I lose my footing, but he falls backward, dropping the scythe with a heavy clank. I fall with him and he wraps his arms around me, in an attempt to keep me from hitting the ground. My wings spring up and wrap around us both. Good thing I can depend on them! We both glance to the side as items fall and shatter to the ground. The shaking lasts for what feels like an hour. A glass pitcher on the bar top falls over and shatters into a million pieces right next to our faces. We huddle on top of each other as the ground vibrates us over to the wall.

"What the hell is that?" I yell.

"I don't know!"

A minute later, the quaking stops. My chest heaves and I place my hand on his pecs to move myself up, fully aware of him . . . and our position. I carefully climb off him, momentarily straddling him. My wings retract back to their usual spot inside my back.

"Whatever that was . . ." Ambrose gets up. "It wasn't good." My eyes scan the bar and look out the window. An earthquake in Florida? Fat chance that's what it was . . .

"Astronomical. They probably felt it down in LLAPS."

My gut drops. "What did you say?"

"Well, that was no regular earthquake . . . We should get back and see what happened ASAP." My face grows pale, and I take out the hourglass. My mouth drops as I hold it up. All the sand has gone down.

"We're too late. The angels are here."

ANGEL BOMBS

ADDISON

When we arrive back at the LLAPS training room, or at least that's what I'm calling it, the reapers are still practicing their various forms of magick. Before getting here, we took a quick gander of what surrounded the bar but there weren't any signs of an army marching down, or angelic activity. To be honest, things were quiet. If it wasn't for our sense of impending doom due to the quake, Ambrose and I would have kept unhypnotizing demons and capturing prisoners.

"You're back." My brother makes his way between reapers throwing ice balls at each other. I rub my arms as a bit of frost reaches me and start toward my brother. He wraps his arms around me and lifts me up.

"You're in a good mood," I say. I catch a glance over his shoulder where Blaise is standing. Ah.

"Yeah well, things are looking up, aren't they?" I quirk a brow.

"Did you guys not feel the giant quake down here?"

"Oh, that?" He rubs the back of his head. "Um yeah, we did."

"Not exactly looking up then."

"Right . . . sorry."

Blaise walks toward us, her eyes pointed directly at me. Why do I get the feeling I know what she's about to tell m—

"So, your angel friends are here now."

"They're not my friends. I don't even know them."

"Well, your mother is one of them, so I'm calling them your friends."

"Hey, take it easy on my sister, will you?" Dax shifts to one leg. "Neither she nor I knew where our mother was, but most importantly, we didn't know a thing about HAPS. OK?"

Blaise's cheeks flush and she tucks a strand of hair behind her ear. "Sorry. I'm just worried."

"I know. Don't worry, we will make sure your people are okay. How bad can the angels be, anyway? And Mom's involved? I'm sure they're just here to help."

"It didn't sound like she wanted to help though, Dax . . ." I mutter.

"Well, what did she say exactly?"

"She was kind of hinting at hitting the restart button on everything. Killing all reapers, demons, prisoners . . . Wiping out LLAPS and starting over in the way they wanted to."

"A total raid," Blaise finished. Dax raises his brows and whistles. I steal a glance over to Ambrose, who's calling a meeting with the reapers. They circle around the Akashic waters, my father included. Dax and I exchange glances and the three of us join the rest of them. I pick a spot beside my father and Evander while Ambrose stands at the far end, swirling the end of his scythe in the water.

"How's the training going?" I whisper.

"Surprisingly well, considering they've all come into their powers. Ambrose had some . . . let's just say, unorthodox methods to train them fairly quickly."

"Unorthodox methods? Ambrose?"

Evander shrugs. "Yeah, he had me scare the daylights out of them until their powers emerged." He chuckles at the end of it. Jeez! "What came after that was just them practicing using their power. Invoking it at will. There aren't many of them, but they at least have this as an advantage over the other reapers.

"Have you heard anything from Sidhe?" I ask.

"Only that they closed their portal. Just like here. No one can get in or out. The angels that got in are being held captive for questioning." My mouth drops. I wonder which angels . . . More importantly . . . was my mother one of them?

"Don't worry, your mother wasn't with them." That's a relief.

"So, what's going to happen now?" Dax whispers.

"Now, Sidhe waits for my command to come down here and take on the angels. They know we've been expecting them, and we can't let the angels do what they intend. They won't stop here, and we'll be next." I gulp. This is going to turn into one giant war between reapers, dragons, and angels. And the demons are the casualties.

"We cannot let this happen on Earth," I say. "We're going to have to lure Lorcan here."

Evander looks at me out of the corner of his eyes. "I fear you might be right."

Clouds surface the water's reflection in front of us. A view of Earth comes into focus. Ambrose dips his scythe and the images enlarge until it's focused on South Florida. He enlarges it again and areas of demonic activity come better into view, rippling waves into the water. We all peer closer in, studying the water like it's a map.

"Still no sign of Lorcan's army," Evander says.

"Where do they go?" I ask. "Why not just end everything now if he's that powerful?"

"I guess he doesn't really have to do anything, considering he created a contagion that hypnotizes everything and creates human zombies," Dax says. That's true. Guess he's watching from his pocket dimension. I wonder what kind of promises he's made to the other reapers.

"Any signs of the angels?" Blaise asks.

Ambrose zooms in again, narrowing his eyes. "They're reconning."

"What do you mean?" I ask.

"It's the only reason they haven't made a move yet. They're surveilling the area, probably waiting for the best location to lure Lorcan out and take him out in one go."

"Right, taking out isolated demons won't be enough to stir Lorcan out of his pocket dimension. They'll want to take out half an army," Evander adds.

"Wait right here." Ambrose zooms back in and an image of someone wearing a white and gold breastplate, alone, comes into view. No doubt that's an angel. The angel approaches a demon. I hold my breath. After a few seconds, the angel turns and walks away.

"What the hell was that? He didn't do anything . . ."

"That's curious," one of the reapers says. Ambrose zooms out to a few inches beside the demon, where there's another, and another. He zooms out more and there's a swarm of demons now.

"Right, that's big enough to—"

BOOM!

Rubble falls from the high-arched stonework of the training room. The ground shakes once beneath my feet and I grab my brother's and Evander's arms.

"Sorry." I let go and straighten myself up. "Is that the boom we were waiting for?"

"That was an angelic bomb."

"A what—"

"That's an oxymoron," Dax says.

"Yes it's filled with a poisonous sleeping gas. It's instant."

"You said sleeping gas . . . Is it fatal?"

"Yes. It makes them want to go to sleep, but once they do, they die. It's fatal to everyone."

"They've started," Blaise says. I hover over the water and see demons dropping down to the ground on their spots, falling asleep to their death.

"Why not just kill them?"

"This way it's easier to clean up. HAPS has always been . . . diplomatic in their dealings." Evander steps away from me and moves closer to Ambrose.

"They call that diplomatic?" I whisper to my brother. He shrugs and shakes his head.

"We should get there before Lorcan shows up," Evander suggests, reaching Ambrose. "But we need to strategize. If we show up now, they'll just bomb us."

Shit. That's a good point. "What should we do?"

"Send Addison down first," Blaise says. Ambrose snaps his eyes to her and so does my brother.

"Absolutely not."

"Hear me out. Her mother should be down there. They're not going to kill her."

"Hell no. My sister is a demon. If Mom doesn't see her right away, she can still be killed by an angel—or Lorcan may show up and take her out."

Blaise is right. If I can get through to my mom, explain to her that we had figured out how to fix everything, and that we just needed more time, I can get her to listen. "I'll go."

"What?" Ambrose walks over to me. "It's too dangerous."

"I know my mom. I can get her to listen. Let me go. It'll make things easier if they leave, or help us," I add. "What if they can help us instead of killing everyone in LLAPS?"

Blaise snorts and I shoot her a look.

"What's so funny?"

"Angels hate LLAPS. This was the excuse they needed to come down and exterminate you guys."

Evander shrugs a shoulder. "I agree with Blaise. It doesn't help that there's a new Judge and they don't know Ambrose."

"In that case, it's only fitting that I too go with Addison. Meet the general and introduce myself."

"I'll go too," Dax says.

"Well, now it's a party. I thought the point was for me to go discreetly?"

"Hey, I want to see Mom! It's only the three of us."

"That's okay. The three of us can go," Ambrose says. "But the rest stay close, beneath the veil. In case Lorcan shows up . . ."

"And shit hits the fan?" Dax says. Ambrose furrows his brows and smacks himself in the face.

"What do I do?" my dad asks.

"You stay here manning the waters," Ambrose tells him.

"Alright. I'm going to work on a sigil I was working on to protect Earth once this is over."

"The sigils you have at home?"

He nods. "I can replicate them here."

I furrow my brows. If he can get that to work, he can stop anything nefarious from ever leaking through the veils again. Permanently.

"What do we do if Lorcan does show up?" Clove asks. "Do we all just go in at once?"

"No, wait for my signal. In case the angels do blow us all up, we need you there as a backup team. Having everyone there at the same time might give them the chance to take us all out with one bird." He winks at me.

I smack my face and pull him away. "Let's go."

HI MOM, MEET MY REAPER

ADDISON

I glance behind me as we step into the portal. The last person I see is Blaise closing it behind us. We land in the center of dozens, if not hundreds, of dead demons. Months ago, I wouldn't have cared about losing them, but now . . . now, things are different. Despite me not wanting to take up the mantle, and not particularly liking all demons, something in me has changed. I mean, yes, duh, I became one, and to be honest, I wouldn't want to give up these powers now. Not because I love power, but because I feel like they belong to me now. Maybe they make me feel like a badass, okay? But also, I have a newfound understanding of what demons went through growing up in LLAPS, how they're forced by their own society to believe they are unwanted and unloved, conditioned into believing they have to do heinous things. When some, deep down, aren't that way at all.

"How do we find mom out here?" Dax asks.

"That's a good question . . . follow the bodies, I guess."

"Right . . . in which direction?"

Ambrose twists a dial on the upper end of his scythe. "I've set it to find angels instead of demons."

"It can do that?"

"It can find anyone, and anything," he says. "They're close."

I swallow. It just hit me that my boyfriend—er, ex-boyfriend—is about to meet my mother for the first time. Well, this may or may not be awkward. Here goes nothing.

I step over a dead body. "I hope they didn't take out all of them . . ."

"They didn't. The angels are lurking around us. They're still here, baiting Lorcan."

"Do you think he'll come?" Dax asks.

"It's a mystery to how Lorcan is playing his game. I fear that if he doesn't come straight away, what's to stop him from skipping town and focusing his efforts elsewhere? He can multiply his army by the tens of thousands if he gets stronger."

I gasp. "Ending Earth a lot quicker," I finish.

"Precisely."

I step over another demon and almost lose my footing. Ambrose catches my hand before I trip over one of their wings. I quickly clasp my hand with his and catch my balance. My stomach does a mini somersault. I look up at him and half-smile. For a few seconds, I don't let go, but as it becomes awkward to walk, I free my hand away from his.

"The scythe is pointing to that chapel up ahead."

"Really? A church?" How very biblical of them. The dead demons lessen as we near the white building with three large crosses in front of it. "I thought HAPS wasn't about this 'God.'"

"They're not entirely. Some of the stories have merit to them, but a lot was lost in translation and recording. They value their belief system, even though it isn't entirely accurate."

"Interesting . . ." I let the silence linger as I ponder what could be accurate and what was left out of belief systems of today. We walk side by side over the sidewalk and onto the sandy grass front of the chapel. Two angels guarding the door come into view.

"Speak your purpose, reapers," one says, then his eyes fall on me. "You . . ."

"Me?"

The angels glance at one another. "The general has been expecting you."

The general? I gulp. It's an odd thing to hear in reference to my mother. They move their lances to their side and the door opens, letting me through. They bar the door again with their lances right after I walk in, blocking out Ambrose and Dax.

"Wait. They're with me."

"Speak your business, reapers. I won't ask again."

"My mother's in there," Dax says.

"And I'm High Judge of the Reaper Council. I wish to discuss our plan moving forward with your general."

They glance at each other again. One of them purses his lips.

"Surely, you want to discuss bringing peace, rather than an annihilation?" Ambrose adds.

"We have no business speaking to reapers," the guard to the right says.

"It's alright, gentlemen." I know that voice. I spin around to my mother standing behind me, wearing the same breastplate she wore when I saw her in HAPS. "Let them through. If the reaper wishes to speak of peace, I have to allow it."

"Very well, commander."

Commander? I knew she was *a* general, but I guess I didn't realize—she's *the* HAPS general. The head honcho in charge.

My nerves settle. See? I knew my mother had more sense than Blaise accounted for. She puts her hand on my cheek and softens her eyes at me, then she walks past me and walks straight to Dax.

"My son. I missed you so very much, please come inside."

Ambrose and Dax crowd the chapel entrance, and the guards slam the heavy doors shut behind them. A soft light from the bulbs on top of the chapel plus the lit candles at the far end illuminate the space. Outside, the sun is setting through the windows.

"Come into the light where I can see you better," she tells him. Dax walks over slowly. A tear wells up in his eye and I swallow to keep mine down. With all the excitement going on and constantly having to move fast, I forgot to imagine how this moment would be. Dax has been dead, but lately to me, he's been alive. I move in closer as Dax wraps his arms around mom and holds her tight. Stepping closer, my mom holds out her arm for me to join. And for a few moments, I close my eyes and enjoy a family hug. I feel Ambrose staring and probably uncomfortable. I clear my throat and pull away.

"We came to talk."

"I know. Let's talk away from them."

I glance over my shoulder to the angels lurking around, pretending not to listen and stare. They had moved all the church seats off to the side and made the space into a camp.

"Is this all of you?" I ask.

"No, there are more of us. Some are still in HAPS. Some

in Sidhe, and others are patrolling the area. They take turns."

"Ah . . ." I see. I turn to Ambrose and hold out my arm. "Mom, this is . . ."

"So, you are Ambrose." She cuts in front of me and holds out her hand. He takes it and she grips it firmly and shakes it, holding his gaze for a moment too long. Oh, this isn't going to be awkward at all.

"It's lovely to meet Addison's mother," he says.

My mom drops his hand and leads us to the back of the chapel, raising her chin while keeping an eye on him in passing. She walks us into a secluded room and shuts the door.

"I know why you're here," she starts. "And we're not backing off. I gave you twenty-four hours, Addison. You're my daughter and I love you. But believe me, this is way over-due. It's time HAPS intervenes." My stomach drops. She didn't even let any of us get a word in.

"But mom.. . . ." Dax starts. "HAPS is killing everything. We just need to take Lorcan down and get the prisoners back to the prisons."

"It won't be enough. Silas"—she clears her throat—"the previous Judge, made a bargain with us to control the cycle and to keep the peace among angels and demons. Now he's gone, and frankly, demons should never have been given any reign." She eyes Ambrose from top to bottom.

"While I may agree that the demons should not have been given reign . . . " I snap a look at him, and he reddens. ". . . back then . . . given who was in charge." Oh, right.

"I do not agree that they do not have the right to live. Killing everyone, including the reapers, is not the answer."

She squares her jaw and peers into his eyes. "Tell me, Ambrose, what is in it for you?"

He tilts his head. "Excuse me?"

"You can't tell me that you, as a reaper, care about the others. Nor the well-being of the demons."

"Let me remind you that your daughter, whom I love very much, is now a demon," he hisses. I swallow.

"Yes, my daughter and son will be joining us in HAPS when this is all over."

"No, I won't," I say. "I do not regret becoming who I am now."

"Do you truly think your angels will accept her as one of them? And her unborn child?"

"Mom . . . You can't really be . . ." Dax trails off as she interrupts him.

"They will accept them both, because I will command them."

"What about Dad?" Dax asks.

"Your father can choose to come with us, but as someone who practices the dark arts, I cannot be accountable for his actions."

"Sounds pretty hypocritical to me," I blurt. My mother snaps her gaze to me. "What did you say?" I continue. "You'll be accountable for my actions, but not my dad's?"

"It's his magick that tainted your blood to begin with," she snaps. Ouch! "And you, reaper, you say you love my daughter. How is it that you know about love anyway?"

Ambrose searches her eyes, pausing for a moment. Is he going to tell her about what he saw in the Akashic? About the other reapers coming into their powers? "I, unlike the others, developed empathy. I can truly say with all my heart that I am in love with Addison." My chest tightens. I swallow the lump forming in my throat. Our eyes meet and suddenly my heart is thumping in my ears. Blushing, and refusing to smile, I look away from him and focus on Dax instead, who hasn't looked away from our mom.

Her lips form a thin line.

"What about Sidhe?" I interrupt their silent standoff.

"What about it?"

"Seriously? Is it necessary to raid the dragons to take their water?"

"Their water? That water doesn't belong to them. They want to guard it instead of letting it flow freely and infinite."

"Wait a minute, you raided them only after Lucifer tainted the waters in HAPS. That's the only reason."

"And now we need more, but they need to recognize a new world order." I cringe at *new world order.*

"And calling a meeting with them wasn't on your agenda? You had to send troops to raid instead?" Ambrose hisses.

Woah . . . This conversation is getting heated. My stomach does a little flip and one of the light bulbs on the corner of the room goes out. I jump and place a hand over my stomach. I think all this stress is making the baby nervous.

My mother looks up at the light and then down at me. "You're going to need better support than what LLAPS can offer you. That was the baby, wasn't it?" Dax snaps a look to me and my face reddens as I rub my tummy, trying to calm it down.

"She'll be fine," Ambrose says.

My mom licks her lips. "Who said it was a raid, anyway?" she says, going back to the last conversation. I quirk a brow. "The moment we went in, my troops were seized and held for questioning. They didn't even get a chance to speak, let alone sit down for a chat."

Ambrose leans on his scythe. "Perhaps they thought an

entire troop showing up unannounced meant a raid and took precautionary actions."

"Why all this hate toward the dragons anyway? Over water? Seems ridiculous," I add.

"Over who controls the Akashic," Ambrose mutters under his breath.

I sigh. I need to diffuse this before it blows out of proportion. More than it already has. "So, what now?"

"Now, it's up to you." She looks at Ambrose with judging eyes. "I'll even include you, Ambrose, since my children are so fond of you and would never forgive me if I were to incinerate you. You three can join forces with us. Come to HAPS. Leave LLAPS behind. After this is all done, we will extend our terrain anyway."

"Extend your terrain after everyone is dead?" Dax says.

"No, I will not abandon my reapers," Ambrose asserts himself, drawing in his scythe.

"Nor the dragons," I add.

"Mom . . . are you listening to yourself?" Dax asks.

She steps back. "Have it your way. I'll do my best to keep my troops from killing you three, but you're on your own with Lorcan. We have a job to do and can't be watching over you when he's here."

My mouth drops. Blaise was right. My chest tightens. I can't believe it. She was right . . . My mother is different . . .

"Mom . . . I . . ." I stutter.

A banging comes from the door.

"What is it?" she demands.

The door swings open and a guard pokes his head in. "Ma'am, Lorcan and his army have arrived."

"Excellent, move the troops."

Ambrose and I exchange glances.

"Time for us to go too, then," he says.

"Mom," Dax starts, "can't we unite forces? The angels and the reapers? Even the demons! Addison has been able to get through to them . . . No one else has to die. We can coexist. This is madness!"

She shakes her head. "My decision has been final. It's time for a reset. A deep purification of the waters is needed, and we can't do that with demons and reapers in the way, controlling everything down below."

I grab Dax's hand. "Forget it. Let's just go."

"But—"

I pull him out of the tiny room, and we walk in silence out of the chapel while the angels gear up and stare at us from the sidelines.

"Wow." Dax's face is grim in the setting sun. "Death has really changed her. Glad that didn't happen to me."

"Death changed you a little bit," I say.

"Not like that."

Dax used to be the life of the party, always making a joke at someone's expense, and reckless, oh so reckless. Since he died, he's matured. A lot. He's kept some of his sense of humor though. I wouldn't know what I'd do if he hadn't. It feels good to have my brother back, but if he had lost all of himself . . . like my mom has . . . it just wouldn't be the same.

The doors behind us swing open. We move over to the side and allow the angel army to march the streets of dead demons.

"Are we just letting them go?" Dax asks.

Ambrose turns a dial on his scythe. "We don't have a choice. Come on, I've called reinforcements. Lorcan's army is about a mile north of here."

We make a left turn away from the angels and take a different route. It would be too weird to walk with them after that conversation with my mother.

A portal opens when we reach a back alley and Blaise and Evander come out, leading our reapers behind them. My eyes sweep past Blaise. I don't want to discuss the conversation with my mother, and I certainly don't want to hear "I told you so." Dax reaches out to her and turns to walk in silence. Ambrose instructs the reapers to group into a formation.

"Are we going into battle?" Evander asks Ambrose.

"Unknown, but better be prepared."

"What happened with the general?"

I wait to hear a response, but when I don't get one, I crane my neck to look at Ambrose. I must have missed a pass of expression between the two of them. I guess he doesn't want to speak negatively about my mother in front of me. Ugh, this whole situation is awkward. Skadi comes running from between the reapers and I reach for her.

"Oh, Skadi, I'd rather you would have stayed behind."

"Sorry," Evander says. "I didn't know what you wanted to do with her, and she seemed eager to come out."

"It's fine, I guess. I just don't want her to get killed." But if we get bombed, we'll all get killed, so . . .

BOOM

I grab onto Skadi's fur and snap a look at Dax, then Ambrose. Heavy clashing of metal erupts a street over, where the angels are.

"Lorcan. It's time. Move out." Ambrose gives his command, and the reapers disappear into portals, only to emerge on the other side. I fall into step with the dragons, Ambrose, and my brother, and follow suit.

Ambrose pushes my head down as a sword nearly

beheads me. I back up into him, and we both lunge out of the way. A blaze of fire heats my face as my brother's arms turn to flame.

"Addison, stay close!" Ambrose calls out and raises his scythe in defense to a reaper (not on our side) lunging their scythe at him. He blocks their scythe. He kicks up, sending them falling backward.

"Why didn't you kill him?"

"I'm not trying to hurt the opposing reapers if I don't have to. I'm hoping they'll change once they see Lorcan's plan fail—"

The reaper gets up and swings his scythe to Ambrose's neck. Before it hits, Ambrose jabs the pointed end of the curved blade straight through his robes. A second later, the reaper turns to ash, taken by the midnight breeze. I flick toward Ambrose.

"They betrayed you, Ambrose. Don't feel bad." I guess empathy is a tough thing to have in these situations. Ambrose doesn't speak for a second and then turns to me.

"We need to unhypnotize demons, get them back," I say.

"I'm not sure that's the priority right now."

"Well, it's my priority. This is how we clean up Earth. And I can't help with the reapers."

"Fine. We split up for the time being. Just be careful."

I nod and search the streets through the fighting between angels and Lorcan's army, scanning for hypnotized demons. At this point, there probably isn't a demon that's not hypnotized. This stupid battle is delaying my mission. I could really use Ambrose's help for range.

A gargoyle perches himself up on top of a building. Same one? I squint. No, the other one had red veins on his horns, this one's veins are blue. I sprint from the fighting to the side of the building, trying not to be seen. How do I get him down here?

"Hey!" I yell. Too much noise, it can't hear me. Also, he's hypnotized. I find a piece of rubble in a corner and pick it up. Swinging it, I throw and hit, missing his foot by an inch. Shit.

A different piece of rubble falls over my head. My wings shroud over my head and I duck to the floor. Peeking through them, I see the gargoyle land on the asphalt with a crash, then quickly jump to his feet. I jump back and crane my neck to see what caused him to fall like that. An angel, with broad wings covering his upper torso and face, jumps down from the roof, landing with a stylish thud. My eyes flick between the angel and the gargoyle.

Do I take him on by myself? Me versus an angel? There's probably a 98.9 percent chance I'll fail. What was it Azazel called them? A terminator army? The way I see it, I can muster up some magick, take on this bad boy by myself . . . and the gargoyle will escape or try something stupid. Or, the angel kills me. So, I don't move.

He doesn't seem to notice me, or doesn't care. The gargoyle doesn't move. What's he doing? I would expect the gargoyle to try and attack the angel, but he just stands there, staring. I thought all hypnotized demons were set to kill anyone not in Lorcan's army. Is this how he attempts to hypnotize an angel?

The angel steps closer to the gargoyle and places his hand between the gargoyle's eyes. I stay frozen solid, my breath shallow as I try not to make a sound. What the hell is going on? Why hasn't the angel blasted the gargoyle to bits yet?

My mouth drops as the gargoyle's eyes turn from milky

to black. He unhypnotized him! But I thought they were here to kill everyone.

"Hey!" I try to call him, but he turns away, his wings spreading as he jumps up and flies, a gust of wind tousling my hair as I watch him take off.

*D*id that just happen? My eyes fall over to the gargoyle who recoils away from me the moment he notices me looking at him. "No, no, it's okay . . ." I open my hand. "Come, it's okay." He tilts his head. "You need to get out of here. Don't get close to anyone. And do not let Lorcan's army see you." He grunts. I turn and open a portal to the prisoner's pocket dimension before he gets turned again. The gargoyle looks at me and then to the portal. "Just trust me, okay? You can't stay here." He looks at me, then to the portal. "Go!" He leaps over my head and disappears into LLAPS. Well, that one is safe at least.

I dash to the edge of the building, looking both ways at the battle still going on. One of Ambrose's reapers unleashes a wave of I don't know what. I'm hit with an invisible force that sends me flying off in the opposite direction. My back hits the wall hard as my wings shield me from most of the blow. I scramble onto my knees and get up quickly, not waiting for another hit.

As I search for Ambrose, my brother comes into view. A

fireball flies toward more of the reapers, catching some of them on fire. From what I understand, his fire won't kill them, but it's enough to stop them. Through the ignited reaper bodies, Lorcan flies overhead, his eyes fully white. Demons form a wall behind him as the reapers fight each other. Angels attack them from behind. As a few angels try to reach Lorcan, he turns, takes out my dagger, and incinerates them. Holy shit. I didn't know the dagger could do that . . . Or was that because he's combined his soul-eating power with it? That must be it. The angels don't even stand a chance against him. Suddenly, despite my newfound power, I feel useless. There's no way I can reach all those demons and without Ambrose's range. Hope is leaving me.

Blaise or Evander sweeps overhead, dragon fire exterminating a row of angels. I gasp. My mom! My legs start to move, and they stop. Demons and reapers had also caught fire.

From the corner of my eye, I see a gold reflection. I turn quickly, hoping to see Ambrose's scythe, but catch the glare of an angel breastplate instead. The angel reaches in for a device. A bomb, no doubt.

I have no idea where my mother is or if she even cares that I'll get caught in the crossfire at this point, but I'm not going to take a chance. This angel is about to pull the trigger and I can't let that happen. I'll deal with the dragons after. I raise my hands and vines grow from the ground, gripping the angel's ankles. The bomb gets pried out of the angel's hand as another vine enters his mouth, gagging him. Eyes bulging, he squeezes the vine with his hands, trying to pull it out of his throat. He can figure that out on his own, not my problem. I turn back to the fight.

Ambrose backs away as he spots me, wrinkles circled around his eyes. He's as much at a loss as I am. There's no way around this. Reapers and demons are dying. I start toward him when movement a few feet away catches my attention. I flick my gaze to a white and gold uniform running between a building. The angel that saved that gargoyle. I look at Ambrose and then back to the angel disappearing into the shadows. I need to get answers. Why did he save the gargoyle? Is there another plan? Another way out of this mess? Giving one uncertain look to Ambrose, whose features are scrunched up in confusion as he looks at me, I dart after the angel.

"Addison!" He calls out my name, but I ignore him. I'll catch up to him later. Right now, I have to find this angel. I jump over a demon's corpse and sprint between the building, zigzagging between some cars parallel parked on the side of the road. I turn the corner and see the reflection of his breastplate turning another corner.

"Hey! Where are you going?" I call out. "I just want to talk; I'm not going to try and hurt you!" Not sure if that last bit makes a difference to him. Not sure I *can* hurt an angel. But I thought it was worth mentioning that I'm not chasing him to fight. I reach the end of the alleyway and turn the corner. He's gone. What the hell? I look up to the top of the building. Nope, gone. Shit.

Something flies overhead, and heat singes the top of my hair. My wings cover me as I duck. This is getting old. I crane my head from within my wings and peek out. A dragon. I need to stop them before they kill one of us. I'm starting to see why they were banned.

I sprint to the end of the alley to see where it landed, but I duck again as another dragon chases the one that just flew past. What the hell? Dragon fire blows through the air in the direction of the lead. What are they doing? The other dragon turns its head. I can't tell if that's Blaise or Evander.

Which one is silver and white and which one is white with iridescent scales? I can't tell them apart when they're in their dragon form. Sue me.

The dragon being chased—silver and white—takes a hit and spirals to the ground, landing hard on top of a bank. I gulp. A tree nearby catches fire and so does the bank. One of them is going to kill the other! But—they're cousins. No, I can't let this happen! Forgetting about the angel for now, I sprint across the street with the other dragon flying overhead. Spreading its wings, it takes off in the opposite direction and I run into the rubble.

"Hello?" I yell. Coughing emerges from the smoke and fire. I shield my face with my arm, and my wings spread out, creating a protective umbrella. I remember first meeting Blaise. She was perplexed as to why her fire didn't burn me. I mean, it's hot as hell, but my wings do protect me.

"Addison?" Evander's voice comes through the rubble.

"Oh my god, Evander?"

"Addison, I'm okay. Let's get you out of here!" His eyes sweep over me. "How come you're okay?"

"I don't know, Blaise asked the same question when she first met me. Hold on." I spread out my hands and water starts emerging from the walls of the falling building, and from the sky. "I think my magick type protects me from dragon fire."

"Well, that's evolutionary," he says, his eyes wide with disbelief.

"So, that was Blaise? What the hell has gotten into her?"

"Yes, she . . . Lorcan . . ." he tries to say, out of breath. "Come on, we have to get out of here. It's too late."

"What? Too late for what?"

"It's too late for Blaise," his voice falters.

"What?" We step over rubble, as I help hold him up. He

got badly bruised from the fall. Wind pushes me back, and I hold steady with my wings. Blaise is back. She flies down and lands in front of us. Inches from my face, she pushes herself against me, her large eyes meeting mine, and I gasp.

They're milky white.

DRAGON FIRE STILL HURTS

ADDISON

"Umm . . . Hey there, Blaise . . ." I stick my palms out in front of me, facing her as she slowly and swiftly moves one giant foot in front of the other. I gulp. "Blaise . . . it's me . . . Addison." Which I'm sure she knows, but we weren't the best of friends either, so . . . Crap.

"Blaise!" Evander calls out. She had tried to kill him too, so I don't think it matters.

"Blaise . . . please, I don't want to use magick on you . . ." I take a step back, almost tripping over a piece of rubble. She snuffs smoke out of her nostrils, her eyes white, narrowing in on me as she pushes me back. "Blaise . . . let me just . . ." I force a foot forward, trying to touch her nose. Fire descends out of her mouth and my wings wrap around me again.

"It's not going to work, Addison!" Evander shouts.

"I have to try!"

She roars in my face, my cheeks pulling back as her spit and smoke splat me in the face. Gross. Jeez, you don't have to yell. I sidestep over to my right, closer to Evander, who grabs my arm and pulls me toward him.

"We have to go. This is a losing battle. We have to regroup."

"What?" I whisper, looking past him to the war zone that is Key West. Smoke billows over shadowy figures battling it out with each other. Reapers and angels zigzag in chaos as some wield scythes while others use magick. And Lorcan nowhere to be seen.

"Now, Addison, let's go. Ambrose and your brother will meet us there. We have to put a different lock on the portals or—" Dread chokes in my throat. Blaise will get in and destroy everything.

"So we're just leaving her?"

Blaise breathes fire at our direction, jumps above us, and descends in a violent crash. The ground shakes and the pavement splits beneath our feet. Almost losing my balance, I grab onto Evander's arm as we try to run from her.

"Get on my back!"

"What!"

"Now!" Evander shifts to dragon form while tossing me on his back. I grab onto his silver-streaked mane along his large neck as he lifts us off the ground. Holy shit balls! We're flying! We fly toward the battle and I try to catch a glimpse of Dax or Ambrose . . . or any reaper I recognize. But I don't. My stomach drops.

Lorcan emerges below, floating himself up toward us. Shit. If he catches up to us, he'll hypnotize Evander too. Then we're really goners. Evander charges toward him.

"What are you doing?"

Fire rushes from his nostrils and I press my cheek to his back as it causes his body to swing. He takes a sharp left and Blaise meets us at the opposite end. I crane my neck to see if Lorcan had caught fire, but he hadn't. Shit. Is he dragon fire-proof too? Evander makes a swift right, gaining speed. Good thing I hadn't had a bite to eat in hours, or I'd be puking all over his back.

Blaise breathes a long gust of fire at us just as Evander swoops down to try to lose her. I think he's trying to make enough space for us to open a portal and have it close before she can get through. She also picks up speed. This time, Evander spins around and breathes fire right at her. Her snout catches fire, and my eyes widen. Oh no. Blaise backs up in the air, her wings carrying her backward. Evander doesn't waste time; he quickly turns back around and continues gaining distance.

A powerful force of red magnetism lunges us upward like a wave. Evander's wings falter and I think we're going to fall. I grab on tighter to his mane and squeeze my eyes shut. I open one eye to see where the hell that came from and notice Lorcan following us, his hands extended. He must be using a forcefield to catch us off balance. I flick my wrist and push a field of magnetism back at him. Two can play at that game. My dagger, my magick, bitch.

Out in front of us a portal opens. As we near it, a tiny fluttering figure hops up and down in the air. I squint my eyes. "Crowley!" We enter the portal at a heart-stopping speed, and before Evander can slow down his pace, we make it into LLAPS, nearly crashing into a high archway. Evander circles around it and slows to a stop. Both my father and Crowley come into view at the top of a hill.

Evander stops next to them and lays down on the gray ground, letting me off. I hop down, my legs wobbly.

"Dad . . ." I draw him in close, hugging him tight. Evander shifts back to human form, his horns now glimmering from the light purple haze LLAPS gives off. My heart is still thumping hard. I'm totally out of breath. I grab onto Evander's shoulder.

"Thanks for what you did back there."

"Yeah, you too."

"Where are we?" I look around my surroundings.

"This is where the ancients used to take off for battle," he informs me and turns to my dad. "Orlando, you saved us at the right moment, my friend."

My dad chuckles. "I know, we were watching you from the waters, waiting for when to open the portal."

"We?" My eyes light up. "Are the others back yet?"

"Yes, they're waiting for us in the training room." He turns, takes out a rune, and draws a sigil in the air. A large hexagonal shape emerges with six smaller circles at each corner, runes spinning inside each. It illuminates a fiery glow in front of us before disappearing. "My protection sigil."

"You did it?"

He nods. "Let's hope it holds." I'm sure it will. He's been working on this for years.

We make it back through the corridors and into the training room where the others are. Reapers are talking all at once, a few are injured on the floor—but we know they'll heal. Others were incinerated and missing. I scan the room and pause on Ambrose and Dax talking in the corner. I run up and give my brother a big hug.

Ambrose lets out a long sigh of relief. "Before your father spotted you and Evander, I was about to go back out . . . I just had to bring everyone in . . ." His voice trails off. "Addie, why did you run from me? This is why I wanted you to stay close."

I let go of my brother and turn to Ambrose's ashen face as he nears me, putting his hands on my arms. My skin tingles at his touch, and this time I let him hold me. My eyes start to sting. I admit I was afraid he was dragon toast.

"I'm sorry—I . . . saw something . . ."

He lifts my chin up and my eyes brush past his lips to his dark, weary eyes. "What did you see?" he whispers.

I'm about to respond when I see Evander limping over to a living space at the far end with three couches and a table at the center. Two reapers help him down on one of the couches as Ambrose, Dax, and my dad follow. I pull away from Ambrose and take his hand to join the others.

"Addie? What did you see?" he asks again.

"Wait a minute." I ask Evander, "How did Blaise get hypnotized? I thought dragons were immune."

"Who said that?" Evander asks without looking up, as one of the reapers tend to his leg.

"Blaise did. She said dragons were immune to demon control."

"Ah yes, demon control. But Lorcan's a reaper."

I knit my eyes together. That still doesn't make sense. "But his power is coming from my dagger—"

"Not all of his power, Addie." Ambrose shifts away from me, sticks his scythe into a patch of gray sand between the stones, and walks over by Evander. He squats down and looks at his knee. "Somehow, Lorcan's power—the one he hadn't developed before taking your dagger—is being forced out of him. We have no way of knowing what that power is exactly, but it's combining with the dagger's power."

I wipe my face and stammer back. "Something I learned right before Deacon died—"

He stops himself as Evander shrinks in his seat, his eyes far away. "He used the dagger to absorb some of the golden scythe's power."

Dax whistles.

I wonder if Azazel meant for that to happen. "So the

dagger is channelling his repressed power and mixing it with its own power plus any power it was able to obtain from when he got close to the scythe."

"Basically, yes. Just like how we all have developed powers out of necessity, Lorcan I'm sure has too. Only we have scythes that are manufactured for a specific purpose. Whereas the dagger was created to be Azazel's all-powerful control weapon."

Dax takes a seat on the ground next to Evander. "But I thought you told me once that no one really knows the extent of a scythe's power?"

Ambrose chafes his chin. "That's true. We don't."

"And it has proven to surprise us, hasn't it? I mean, you used it to heal me once..."

"And failed," Ambrose says.

"But you've healed other things. Maybe you just hadn't developed your power yet. And almost healing me was the start of it."

Ambrose sighs. "What are you implying?"

"I don't know. Maybe the reapers can project their power even more."

"He does have a point," I add. "Just like you added range to my power." My eyes widen and I gasp. He perks up. "Ambrose... you added range to *my* power..." He raises his brows, expecting me to elaborate. "What if you all can join your power together to wipe out Lorcan?"

"That's an idea," Evander says. "But what about the angels? They're not going to give up now that they've decided they want dominion."

"True. Hmm..."

"How many prisoners were you able to save?" Evander asks.

"Just one . . ." I look down at my feet. "Oh, but I didn't unhypnotize him."

"What do you mean?" Ambrose says.

"That's what I wanted to tell you. When I got distracted and ran away . . . an angel saved the gargoyle. Then I opened the portal for it to come here, so it would be safe from being rehypnotized."

Evander and Ambrose exchange glances.

"I'm sorry, what? An angel unhypnotized the demon?" Dax asks.

I nod. "Yep."

Dax raises his brow. "But why would an angel do that?"

"I have no idea. That's why I ran after him."

"We won't be able to beat the angels with our type of magick," Ambrose says after a few moments of us not talking. "The reapers need to rest, and we don't have the manpower or time to fight them." He rests his head on his hand.

"Hey man, we will figure this out," Dax says.

"The biggest problem now is Blaise is under Lorcan's control," Evander says.

"Okay, I think the immediate game plan should be to unhypnotize Blaise," I say. "Ambrose, you and I should go. We can do the same thing we did last time but to a dragon. Just try not to get burnt because—that would be it."

He shakes his head. "Evander, tell her."

I stare at Evander. "Tell me what?"

"Blaise is gone, Addison. She—" His voice hitches.

"What do you mean?"

"We come from a different world. Even though dragons are almost like mortal humans, when we're in dragon form, magick like that cannot be undone."

"No." I shake my head. "I won't accept that." We have to try. Why won't they at least try?

He sighs. "You don't understand. If she had been hypnotized as a human, then yes, we could have saved her. But as a dragon, her mind is more primal. Ambrose already tried to break the spell."

"But *Ambrose* doesn't have the ability to reach her like I do." He scrunches his face at me. "I'm just saying, if I can reach demons, maybe I can reach her. With your help, Ambrose."

"We can try, but it will be very dangerous. Dragon fire will kill me."

"But it can't kill me," I say.

"Yes, I found that interesting," Evander adds. "I'm not sure it's entirely true though."

"What do you mean? You saw how it hit me and my wings blocked it."

"Yes, but without your wings?"

"...I admit it is very hot."

"So, take your wings away and...?"

"But why would my wings be taken away?"

"If Lorcan catches you, he can torture you, cut them off ... and then use her to kill you," Ambrose says grimly. I gulp.

"I still have to try," I mutter. All those people. All those demons...HAPS can't win. Lorcan cannot win.

A knock comes to the door of the training room. We glance at each other and then to my dad. For a second, I thought it was him knocking, but he's been sitting here silently listening to us. Dax and Ambrose stand up. Evander raises his knee, but Ambrose motions for him to stay down.

"Dad? The sigils..."

"You did put up the new warding, didn't you?" Ambrose asks him.

"Yes, I did. I hadn't tested it before this though . . . " Ambrose and I glance at each other and the room grows quiet.

"Reapers be ready," he says. The reapers stand in a U shape, circling the entrance. Ambrose nods at one of them to open the door.

The door widens and my jaw drops. A soldier from HAPS walks right in, his breastplate reflecting off the waters as he enters.

Now that his wings aren't blocking him, I can see his face.

"Lucifer!" I yell. "You?"

"Am I interrupting anything?" He casually walks in, throws his breastplate off, and walks over to one of the couches, plopping himself down.

KNOCK KNOCK, IT'S THE DEVIL

ADDISON

Reapers point their scythes at him as he takes out an apple and bites down.

"You can put those away. I'm not here to hurt anyone."

My lips part and I glance at Ambrose, whose muscles are tense and ready with his scythe. Evander is holding himself up and Dax's hand is on fire. I scan the arena. No one says a word. Nobody moves. Lucifer takes another bite of his apple.

"What the hell?" I break the silence. Ambrose flicks his gaze to me.

"Yes, what the hell, indeed?" Lucifer says. "Why is everyone so stunned? Surprised to see me?"

"You're the one who freed that gargoyle . . ."

Still chewing, Lucifer nods and looks up at me. "Yeah, that's right."

I raise a brow. "Why?"

"What's your game plan?" Dax says.

"That's a stupid question." He swallows. "To unhypnotize my people. Since you're all doing a lazy job at it."

I gasp in a breath and let it out slowly, my hands trembling. "Lazy . . . ? *You left!* And by the way, I opened a portal to let that gargoyle escape. You unhypnotizing it wouldn't have been permanent. The hypnosis that Lorcan created is contagious."

Lucifer quirks a brow and sits up. "That so?" He finishes his apple and throws it on the ground. "Huh."

"Huh? That's all you have to say? 'Huh!'" I sigh.

"I admit, I didn't know that. Well, that was a big waste of my time. What are you all doing about it?"

I shake off his question. "Where have you been? Last I saw you, you were in HAPS!" He claps his hands and straightens up as he snickers at me. "I 'let' them catch me, so I could take them out and steal their uniform. I've been blending in ever since, taking them out from the inside. And my end game"—he looks at Dax—"is to take over HAPS."

"I can't let you do that," Ambrose says. Lucifer chuckles.

"Fine. You think you can stop me, but you'll want me to take over HAPS."

Ambrose rolls his eyes up, keeping his body rigid. "And why is that?"

"Because I'm the best thing that can happen to HAPS. The angels shouldn't be controlling the planes, and you know it."

"And you can do better?" Ambrose responds.

"I was born for the job."

I chuckle. "Right, that's why you were stuck in a cage?"

Lucifer furrows his brows, snaps his gaze to me, and curls his lips to a sneer. He stands. "By a selfish dead man who made himself Judge. He allowed HAPS to have domain." He sits back down. "But you know what?" Without waiting for an answer, he keeps going. "I no longer fault him. I understand why he did it. I understand why he was afraid. But that fear is what kept so many people restricted.

And yes, I know I can do better. But I don't need you to agree with me. It will happen."

I gulp. What will happen? Him taking over HAPS? Great, something else to worry about. Is this really the end of the world? Should we just wave the white flag now and get it over with?

"You need to leave," Ambrose says.

"You need me here. After all"—he shoots me a look —"weren't you looking for me? Didn't you want me to put things back to the way they were so you can go back to doing whatever it was up on Earth?"

He's got a point. I was looking for him. I turn to face Ambrose. "He did rescue a demon . . ."

"Of course he did, Addison. But he never has the world in his best interest. He's self-serving."

"And who told you that? You're just listening to stories."

Silence unsettles the room. With the literal devil in here, any reaper is afraid to move or speak. They all saw what he did to the Judge. And also, he's powerful. Incredibly freaking powerful. If that's what he could do to the Judge . . . we do need his help.

"Ambrose . . . I think we should give him a chance."

"What?" Dax says.

"Addie, you can't be serious."

"He's an archangel! The only one, beside your scythe, who can kill an immortal. We need him to fight against Lorcan and the angels."

"But he wants dominion over the angels *and* here!"

"You're talking like I'd give you a choice in the matter," he says. Ambrose points the scythe to his throat and Lucifer raises his chin and arms, a wide smirk appearing on his face.

"Alright. So, you have my son's chosen scythe. Fine.

Listen, I don't want dominion over LLAPS. I made Addison queen for a reason. Now, my son had been part of that plan, but I understand he's a bit . . . indisposed." I swallow. "But no matter, semantics. We'll figure it all out as one happy family after this is all over."

I curl my lips.

"What do you say?" Ambrose shoots back.

I clench my fists. Happy family my ass. Although, shit . . . he's my baby's grandfather. Fuck me sideways. I mean, I knew it of course, but I didn't think he'd care. Then again, why wouldn't he?

"You're not getting anywhere near the baby," Ambrose hisses.

"Like I said, we'll discuss it later."

I hold my stomach and take a step back. Yep. I'll have to figure out how to kill the devil. My eyes fall to the scythe . . .

"There's something no one is talking about here!" Evander yells, and we all look at him. "My cousin is a hypnotized dragon under Lorcan's control."

"Oh, now that is a problem," Lucifer says.

I grab my head. "It's *all* a problem. Lorcan is eating souls and somehow the dagger is powering this up. He's . . . unstoppable."

"Hmm . . ." Lucifer chafes his jaw. "You know, the person who created that scythe also created the dagger."

"I know," I hiss. "Your son."

"All I'm saying is . . . he's probably the only one strong enough to defeat Lorcan."

"Wait!" Dax bellows. "Azazel didn't die in the blast?"

"No . . . he got transported somewhere . . ." I tell him.

"Absolutely not," Ambrose declares.

I laugh and stare at Lucifer. "Is this what this is about? You're trying to get us to release your son?"

Lucifer puts his legs down and bends forward in his seat. "I know you saw him."

"Then why don't you go get him? I know you know where he is."

He falls silent.

"I mean, why are you even here? He's your son."

Lucifer stretches his jaw. "I can't go there."

My features scrunch. "Why not? Is the devil afraid of the monsters that live in purgatory?"

"Azazel is in purgatory?" Ambrose asks.

 I nod. "Yup."

"And you were with him?" He eyes me inquisitively.

"He helped me get out."

"And you didn't help him get out," Lucifer spits.

"No! Why would I have?" My face grows red. "Also, I thought you wanted him out of the way."

"Because he's the father of your child." He points to my stomach and I guard it again. "And no, me leaving him there was never my intention. Contrary to what you think of me, I do care about my son."

"That's not a good enough reason," I spit.

"I can't go there because I get ejected when I try, and believe me, I've tried. Can't get in without the scythe. I can't touch the scythe. For some reason it transported Azazel instead of killing him. Who knows what that master alchemist had up his sleeves . . ." He trails off. "And it *will be* a good reason when that little bundle of joy gets older and needs their dad."

"The baby will have a father," Ambrose interrupts, and Lucifer raises his chin again. My heartbeat races in my ears as my stomach somersaults. I look at Ambrose and my lips part. My throat clogs up and I clear it. I can't process what he just said. He said it before, but even after I told him I needed space, he still wants to be the baby's father . . .

"Azazel can command the dagger." Lucifer's voice brings me back to the present.

"Why'd he need me to release you then?"

"That had to do with the cage, not the dagger." Oh, that's true. Shit, is Azazel really our only hope? Would he even agree to this? Yes, of course he would. He'd take any chance to get out of that horrible place, especially if it's to be reunited with his father and take over the planes . . . But I can't let him take control of LLAPS. I'll have to make a deal with him. I'll have to hold something over him.

I look down at my stomach. He might just cooperate for this. But then, I'll have to kill him.

"Fine. I'll do it."

Lucifer's eyes light up his chiseled face. A smile spreads over his face.

"Excellent. I'll go back to Earth and handle the angels. I'll take them out one by one, luring them alone. No one has suspected yet. And they won't; I'll make sure of it. I'll also be releasing demons while you're away."

"Addison, no," Ambrose interrupts. "This is madness. It'll only complicate the matter."

"No, Ambrose, Lucifer's right. Azazel is the only one who knows how to defeat Lorcan and the angels. We need him." As much as it pains me to admit that, it's true. I remember from when I fell into the water in HAPS, Azazel had fought them before, and he knows how to defeat them. His eyes search mine.

"I'll come with you."

I shake my head. "No, Ambrose, it isn't easy getting out."

"Actually, you might need the extra manpower. The

scythe will be useful to get you all out, should you face any problems."

"But what if Ambrose can't get out?"

"I will be able to, Addison." He takes my hand. "I have already reached my highest potential, here in these waters."

My lips slant upward. "From learning and accepting who you were?" A glimmer of hope shines in his eyes as he looks at me.

Lucifer claps his hands and stands up. "Shall we get a move on then? You two rescue my son, and the rest of you, come with me."

"No. I won't risk my reapers. They need their rest. Dax, you go with Lucifer; keep an eye on him." My brother nods and lowers his gaze to Lucifer.

"Great!" Lucifer smacks Dax in the back. "We can be besties!"

Dax exchanges a disgruntled glance with Ambrose and then me, grimacing as Lucifer rubs his back.

Ambrose and I walk to the far end of the room and he places his hand on my arm.

"Why don't I go instead?" he says.

"No, he won't trust you. It should be me." Even though I pushed him back last time I saw him . . . he's probably really pissed at me.

Evander walks over to us with a slight limp. "Best to enter that place from Earth, remove the scent of LLAPS from you both."

My eyes widen. "The last time I went, I had left from Earth and the dwellers of that place were still able to sniff me out."

"You best believe it'll be one hundred times worse coming from here. You have demon blood, so they'll be able to detect you, but coming from LLAPS? It'll be like shooting a flare gun the moment you land."

I suck in a breath, remembering my mother saying we give off a smell.

"And leave during their day as well," Evander says.

A shiver runs down my spine. "He's right. Nighttime is more dangerous over there." I remember hiding in the cave while those creatures searched for me, hungry and fierce. "What time is it on Earth right now?"

Ambrose checks a dial on his scythe. "Six hours to sunrise."

I rub my eyes and my stomach growls. Lucifer's half-eaten apple levitates from where he threw it and floats over to me. My mouth drops as I step away from it. Ew.

"I–I didn't do that . . ." I stammer. At least I don't think I did. I didn't mean to. Lucifer quirks a brow and walks over.

"Hungry, Mama?"

I gasp.

"She needs to eat and rest, or she'll be useless fighting angels and saving demons," he finishes.

Evander takes the apple suspended in air and tosses it back to Lucifer. "He has a point."

"Well, we need to leave from Earth anyway. We'll stop at Paradise House first," Ambrose suggests.

I don't argue. The worries of the world are washing over me as a wave of tiredness weighs down on my body. My stomach roars and all I can think about right now is my empty kitchen and my bed.

RECONCILIATION

ADDISON

We step through the portal straight into my bedroom when lightning strikes from outside followed by the clapping of thunder. Looks like we came just in time for a sea storm.

Nausea overwhelms me as I plop down on my bed. Ambrose pulls down the blanket and helps remove my shoes.

"Thanks."

"It's my pleasure. How are you feeling?"

"I'll be okay. Just tired. And hungry."

"I'll go see what's in the kitchen."

"Probably nothing. Some things were rotten when I left. Maybe check the cabinets though."

"If I can't find anything, I'll leave and come back with something."

My eyes are already closing as his voice drifts far away. I curl myself into a ball and fall asleep.

A tapping at the door wakes me and I sit up.

"It's just me." As Ambrose steps through the door, I get a whiff of . . . Oh my god . . . Is that Burger King?

My eyes widen as I grab for the bag. "Where'd this come from?"

"I made a trip to somewhere the apocalypse wasn't bearing down."

My eyes light up. "My hero."

I take the bag, open it, and stick a few fries in my mouth.

"After this is over, I want to take a vacation somewhere, get out of the Keys for a bit. And not go into the astral plane for a long, long time." Ambrose looks down at the bed sheets. Shit. "I mean . . . You could still see me if you want to. You can always . . ." I swallow a sip of my soda. "Open a portal and come see me, you know."

"I'd like that." He sits at the edge of the bed. The silence grows between us, despite the downpour outside, as I take a bite out of my cheeseburger.

"Do you want a bite?"

"No, that's all for you. You should get some more rest when you're done. I've cleared out some zombies and noticed the water in your kitchen . . ."

"Yeah, it's gross, I think something died near the pipes."

"I cleared it out for you as well."

"Really? How?"

He points to his scythe leaning against the wall. Okay, I did not know it could do that, but I guess it makes sense. One sweep of that purple light can clear anything out.

"How long do we have left?" I ask.

"There's still enough time for you to sleep a bit more, if you want." He reaches over to a photo frame on my nightstand, picks it up, and studies it. Me, my brother, and parents are standing in front of Cinderella's castle in Disney. Dax has his hand sticking out, covering my face as I try to fight him away but fail, while he sticks his tongue all the way out to the camera. My mother rolls her eyes in the background while my dad is laughing. "That was at Disney," I tell him. "I think Dax was mimicking a muppet with the face he was making." I chuckle and stick another fry in my mouth.

Ambrose smiles.

"We used to fight a lot, you know, like siblings do. I miss those days."

"It sounds nice." His voice sombers as he puts the photo back.

"Yeah. I wish I could go back in time. Experience that day again."

"You can still have that, you know." His voice is down to a whisper. The air thickens between us as he looks back at me over his shoulder.

". . . Yeah." I take another sip of my Coke and swallow. "So . . . Have you remembered anything else from when you were alive?"

He shakes his head. "No, but I've probably been too preoccupied to reflect on it. Certain things are starting to feel more familiar though."

"Like what?"

"Connections I'm making with other reapers for one. Maybe it's because they're becoming more relatable since they've discovered their memories, or maybe I'm just paying more attention to it now since I'm not pushing down my empathy. But I do feel it's something I've been missing."

"Connection?"

"Yeah, I think so." His eyes rise to mine, and he cracks a smile.

"Well, you have come a long way from the ominous, hard-core reaper I first met. Mr. stab a demon disguised as a person in broad daylight. Didn't think twice. Just took out your scythe and pow." I stab the air with my hand in mimicry.

He scoffs. "Thinking back on that day, that definitely was an odd thing for me to do in broad daylight, wasn't it?"

"You're telling me." I laugh. "Talk about first impressions." Kill my ex-boyfriend, why don't yah? I know, I know, he was one of Azazel demons in disguise. But it's not like I knew that back then. So much has changed. Ambrose has changed . . . I've changed. Hell, even Dax has changed.

"Anything else?" I ask.

"Fear," he says, almost inaudible.

"Fear?" I repeat.

"I never felt it like this before, Addie."

My amusement falters as his eyes settle on me. I scoot closer to him, partly to hear him better, but also . . . Us being sat on the bed like this, chatting away as friends, makes me miss him so much. Even though he's here physically, I miss staying up late when he'd visit between reapings and talking about all sorts of human things he never understood before. "But fear, how?"

He takes a breath. "As a reaper, I'm used to death. Used to me guiding humans to where they need to go on the bridge." His voice grows hoarse, and he clears it. He takes a moment. "After Deacon's sudden death, her death being so much more permanent . . . it made me realize I can lose a lot more than my own life against Lorcan. Or an accident with dragon fire." Silence lingers in the air. I place my hand on his arm and his eyes fall to stare at it, his other hand joining mine.

"I guess," he continues, "being immortal has always been such a safeguard, even though none of us ever thought of it that way." He chuckles. "We never thought of it at all.

There was always the threat of the golden scythe, and the Judge taking one of us out if we got too out of line, except—" He pauses. "That never really happened until I started developing empathy and wanted to save a child. And then your brother . . ." His voice trails off. I sit and listen to him, wondering if he's had a chance to talk about these things with anybody else. "My biggest fear though . . . is losing you, Addie."

My breath hitches. His eyes meet mine and I squeeze his arm. "You know," I say, "I've always loved the way you look at me. From day one, you've always looked into my eyes like I'm the only woman you've ever laid eyes on. Even now, with my . . . changes, you haven't stopped."

"And I never will."

Blushing, I pull my hand back.

We sit in silence for a few more minutes. I look out the window. It's still storming. I ball up the bag and cheeseburger wrapper and kick off the bed.

"Where are you going?" he asks.

"Hell, while I'm here, I might as well shower. Don't know when I'm going to get another chance." I leave him in my bedroom and walk into the bathroom, kicking off my pants and pulling my shirt over my head. "I bet I can make the water boil with my magic. Don't know why I didn't think of that before." I pull my sports bra over my head and toss it to the floor. I turn the knob and open the shower, letting clear, cold water spew out. I warm my hands up and send the heat flowing through the sprocket. Perfect.

I take a palm full of shampoo and start scrubbing my hair, humming to myself. The bottle of shampoo floats in front of me and I smile to myself. "There you are. I forgot you liked my singing, little one." Despite everything, I have become fond of the idea of having this baby . . . I grab the conditioner out of the air and finish lathering myself. As I open the sliding glass door of the shower, I reach for my towel, but it floats off to the other side of the bathroom. Sighing, I step out dripping wet. The doorknob turns and begins to open. I gasp, quickly reaching for the towel and slamming the door.

The lights go out. "Shit, that'll be the power."

"Addie? Are you okay?" Ambrose calls out. My face reddens.

"I'm fine!"

Not that he hasn't seen me naked before . . . Well actually, only semi-clad. Yeah, I don't exactly want to run out butt naked, especially with the state that we're in. I place my hand over my stomach. "You're going to be trouble, aren't you? You mischievous little thing."

"Who are you talking to?"

I chuckle, wrap the towel around me in a tight knot and walk out. "Umm . . . the baby is a bit of a prankster . . . And . . . it likes my singing."

"Ahhhhh, I see. Giving you trouble already, is it? I thought someone got in there with you!" His bemused smirk lights up the room as he taps the scythe to light up a soft purple. A butterfly flutters in my gut. Oh, damn butterflies.

"Looks like the storm cut the power out," he says.

"Mhmm . . ." I briskly walk over to my dresser drawer to pull out a similar set of pants and a shirt. This time, the pants are an army green and a black tank top and belt. I set it on the dresser and pull open my underwear drawer, quickly sorting through my panties and sports bras. I catch a glimpse of Ambrose turning his head quickly and my cheeks blush.

"Umm . . . I'll let you uh, get dressed," he says. I set the clothes down and spin around.

"Wait."

He pauses mid-walk. "Hm?" A thunderclap makes my heart race as I scramble for words.

"This is stupid."

"What is?" Me. I'm stupid, I want to say. Us being apart while you've been so amazing to me. The stupid excuses I've been telling myself about the APB, when I know he was doing what he had to. I was just being selfish. Seeing Azazel's face emerge from his features, well, that one might be true, but I'm getting over that. I think. His mouth parts to speak and before I can change my mind, I erase the space between our bodies and grab his face . . . Resisting him is a losing battle. He sucks in a breath and my lips crush to his.

He gasps for a second and I let go. Then he grabs my neck, pulling me back. We're not in the astral plane, we're at home. I don't have to worry about my surroundings changing like in the mental plane. Or about him changing. I know it's really him. For now, Azazel is tucked away where he can't hurt me. For now. I push that out of my mind and take Ambrose's tongue in mine. My hands spread over his chest, running my fingers over his strong pecs. "I've wanted you for so long," I whisper.

"Oh, Addie . . . Me too . . ." I push him toward the bed, the towel loosening between us till it falls on the floor. Lungs empty, heart racing, I start tugging on his robes and he takes them off while I move down to unbuckle his pants. His eyes drop down to my body and a gust of breath escapes his lips. They stop at my breasts, then to my waist, drinking me in, and then come back to my eyes.

"Are you sure you want to do this?"

"Shut up." I quirk a brow and curl my lip. An oh-so-sexy grin spreads on his face as a lightning bolt backlights his features and he hurries and undresses himself. Finally. And holy shit. Beneath all those robes, he looks like a god.

Suddenly, he picks me up and I squeal, a giggle escaping my throat as he lays me down on the bed. He kisses the nape of my neck, making his way down my chest, tickling my skin softly with his lips as he does.

He grabs onto my hair from underneath and gently pulls and a moan escapes me. He looks down, a twinkle in his eye I'd never seen before, and I can't help but smirk. I place a finger on his lips, and he stops. I grin widely as I scoot out from under him.

"What are you doing?"

"Shhhh . . ." With him in front of me, I push him to lie on his back and climb on top of him. He gasps as I straddle him. He sucks in his breath as I press my lips against his neck. I squeeze my legs around him, pressing myself over his body.

"I want you," I tell him, moving him over my core. And I slide down, bringing him into me. A moan escapes my throat and my eyes roll back. He caresses my breasts and I grab onto his shoulders, digging my nails into his skin as I ride him, filling myself with his girth. He brings himself up so that I'm sitting on him and reaches for my bottom lip with his teeth. My fingers coil between his hair and I tug gently, this time making him moan.

"Oh my god." This was so long overdue. I ride him as slow as I possibly can, teasing him and me . . . and I wrap my hands tighter around him, bringing him in closer, and whisper, "What did you say at the church before?"

He quirks a brow, his eyes moving rapidly at first, then he smiles. "That I'm in love with you."

I bite my lip, still moving back and forth, slowly. "Tell me again."

"Addison, with all my heart, I am in love with you."

I place one hand against his jaw, squeezing slightly as I stare into his dark eyes. "I love you too." And I kiss him.

He grinds into me and I take him in fully. My nails dig into his back as I pick up the pace, thrusting my waist back and forth, riding him harder and harder.

"My reaper," I say, teasing him with a smirk. He lifts off the bed a little, wrapping his arms around me and spinning me back down so my back is against the bed. My eyes are wide as he strokes me deeper and deeper, faster and faster. Until he slows down, pressing his head against mine.

"Addison . . ." His hot breath tickles my neck.

"Mmmm . . ."

"I will never leave you again."

"Shhhh . . ." I wrap my legs tighter around him, drawing him in closer, and he speeds up again. His body shudders as he squeezes his eyes shut, his lips parting, reaching down and groaning against my lips as he finishes inside me with me moaning against his cheek.

He slides out of me and lies down with his hand on my hip.

Pulling away from him, I admire his beauty. His immortality really does make him that much more ethereal. Sometimes I forget. But then again, we're always on the run to or from something.

Sweat beads down my back as I reach for another kiss. I smile, taking in the giddy grin pasted on his face. This was exactly the normalcy I wanted.

"I missed you," I say.

"I missed you so much, Addie. I'm so so sorry."

"Shhhhh . . . Let's not talk about that anymore. Okay?"

"That's fine with me."

I peek over to the balcony. The rain seems to have let out a little and the sun is rising.

"Is it time to go yet?" I say.

He leans back to look at the soft light coming in through the mauve curtains and I trace my finger over his abs. He chuckles. "At this rate, the apocalypse will befall the rest of Earth."

I scoff. "Wow, was that a joke?"

His grin widens as he gives me the side-eye and pulls himself out of bed to check his scythe. "It should be dawn over there now. Why don't you get a little more sleep? We'll leave in an hour." My eyes blink closed.

"Mmmm . . ." Sleep sounds good.

He pulls the sheets over us and I rest my head on his chest, running my fingers over the lines of his pecs. Just as we should be. Finally.

We wake up about an hour or two later and Ambrose opens his eyes and smiles.

"Time to go rescue a dirtbag," I say.

After another shower, I quickly dress and redo my tight braid. I take one last look at my bedroom before I shut the door and Ambrose walks over to my side.

"Ready?" He extends his hand out and a giddy smile crosses my face, my stomach doing flips. I take his hand as if we're about to go on a date to a theme park instead of into the dangerous plane of purgatory where monsters who eat demons will try to kill me.

"I was born ready." I have no idea if he understands that, but he chuckles and turns to the living room.

Ambrose grips his scythe and turns a dial. Moments later, a silver portal opens.

Ambrose and I glance at each other and he holds my hand tight.

"It'll be okay," he says. "As long as we're together, we're going to be alright."

And with that, I lean over and kiss him one more time. Before stepping into the gray ether of purgatory.

TIME TO RESCUE A DIRTBAG

ADDISON

*A*mbrose clutches me under his arms as we land with a thud on the gray grass, under the chilling gray sky. Climbing to my feet, I dust myself off and lend him my hand, helping him up. We're here.

The arid temperature and silence of the plane diffuses my temperament. I had forgotten the effects this place has on emotions and temper, snuffing it out of a person. I wondered whether, after the last time I was here, it would still influence me. Ambrose closes in behind me. I wonder if it would influence a reaper . . . I glance at him. He seems fine.

"Are you alright?" he says.

"I'm fine. How are you feeling?"

He pauses, breathes in deeply, and looks around. "Like what I've recently learned about myself no longer matters." Oh shit. It does affect him. We cannot be here long.

"We have to hurry then. This place . . . it . . ."

"Snuffs the emotion out of you?"

"Yes . . . And I just got you back."

He pulls me into him. "Nothing can snuff out how I feel

about you. Nothing." A smile curls on my face. "But we should hurry anyway."

"Where do we even start looking?" Would he still be hiding out in the cave as a goat? I pull away from Ambrose and take a few slow steps toward the trees. Cautious over the sound of my own breathing, careful not to crack a twig under my feet, and extremely careful not to draw attention to us. "This place is primal," I whisper. "We have to watch it-"

An arrow whizzes past my cheek. I gasp and breakneck to Ambrose. He blocks it with his scythe.

"That was a close one," he says.

"Ambrose . . . The scythe . . . Can you use it here?"

His brows furrow in concentration.

"What are you—"

"Wait."

I pause as he turns a dial all the way up.

"No. It's a dead zone." His face drops. "I never knew that was possible. I'm powerless here."

I nod. "That's what I suspected. Don't worry, I'm not." This is where I reached my highest power, where I killed my most feared self. Another arrow whizzes past us and hits a tree. "We can't stay here in the open. Let's go." I run toward the tree and pull the arrow out; we duck behind the bark.

"We're still very visible," I whisper. Maybe the two of us being here was a bad idea. What if he gets hit? The rules here are different. If they can hurt a demon, can they hurt a reaper? I gulp. I don't want to sit around and find out.

An arrow hits Ambrose in the chest and I yelp.

"Oh my god . . ."

"I'm fine." He pulls it out and I swallow, letting my breath out slowly. Okay, well, he can't really be hurt, and I already know what can kill a reaper, so . . . it'll be okay. I just have to focus on not getting killed.

"Don't worry about me," he says. "Where to?"

I twist my lips and look around. Which way was that cave? I tug on his clothes, beckoning him to follow. It has to be deeper into the gray forest since the clearing is behind us. The last time I was here I ran behind a few trees, and I remember the cave over to the left somewhere. Not the best directions. But it's not like I have a map.

An arrow almost takes off my nose and I still. My eyes move toward the left and I catch movement behind some trees. I create a fireball in my hand, and gasp at its green color. Like the evil version of me had. I throw it over to where I think something's hiding, and it catches the tree in a blazing heap of green flame.

"Come on!" I yell. We dash straight ahead to a giant boulder. "Right over there!"

A growl emerges from behind the boulder, and I stop in my tracks. Ambrose almost smacks into my back. Footsteps come from around us and I duck closer to the ground, stancing myself into position. Ready to fight, I grip the arrow I had pulled from the tree. Come on, you fuckers.

"Looking good."

I grow rigid. That voice . . . My breath hitches.

"How long's it been?"

I straighten myself up and look at Ambrose, who's become noticeably more uncomfortable. He grabs my arm and pulls me close to him.

"Awww . . . Are you two back together? How wonderful."

"Where are you?" I say.

"You'll have to come inside. You know where I am."

"Where is he?" Ambrose's tone is firm and hoarse.

I follow him around the boulder and to the entrance of

the cave. Peering into straight darkness inside. I hold my breath. "Come out."

A few moments pass, and two bright red eyes glow, chest height. Slowing, he walks out, shifting from goat to demon as he comes closer. A sharp dimple hits his left cheek as he stares at me. I raise my chin, still pointing the arrow at his direction. My stomach moves a little and I shift. Shh, no baby, now is not the time.

His chest is bare, and his wings spread out. His irises turn from the glowing red to a deep brown, almost black. His hair falls over his face as he keeps his cynical smile pasted on his lips. That smile I once thought was sexy until I hated it. That smile that still finds its way into my dreams at night until I startle awake and shake it from my vision. That evil, sexy grin of his that still haunts me. Oh, how I hate him. And soon I will have to kill him.

"Addison. You're looking . . ." He sucks in a breath. "Devilish." His dimple presses into his face. "I wondered when you'd come back. If you'd come back. After all, I'm still here because of you." His eyes shift over to Ambrose. "Now you, I can't say I'm happy to see." He comes closer until he's just a few inches from me and I suck in a breath. My stomach turns. I think his presence is making the baby move. I place a hand over it. He slants his smile as he catches me doing that. "And just how is our little bundle of joy?" He reaches for my stomach, and just as I take a step back, Ambrose swings his fist with full force, clocking Azazel right across the jaw.

"Ambrose!" I yell and stifle a laugh. I mean, I don't blame him, but . . .

For a second, Azazel keeps his face in the direction of Ambrose's blow, then cracks his jaw and turns to face him. A second later, Azazel swings. Ambrose blocks his punch.

Holy shit, Ambrose blocked Azazel's punch! I did not know my reaper could fight! He throws another punch but Azazel blocks that one. The scythe hits the floor and I watch, wide eyed, as Azazel and my boyfriend break into hand-to-hand combat. I flinch as Azazel hits Ambrose in the eye and Ambrose lets out a grunt.

"Guys . . ."

Ambrose topples over, catches his balance, and rushes toward Azazel, knocking him straight down as they both hit the ground hard. Looking around, I make sure those creatures aren't anywhere to be seen. This is counterproductive.

"Guys!"

They ignore me. Azazel flips his legs over, sending Ambrose crashing behind him and hitting his back against the rock. He quickly gets up and wrestles Azazel to the ground. His muscles flex through his shirt as his robe is now hanging off to the side. God damn, go Ambrose!

But no, seriously, they need to stop. Ambrose pins Azazel's throat with his left hand and beats him repeatedly with his right fist. Over and over. Blood gushes from Azazel's lips. My stomach makes an unsettling flip. Can Ambrose kill him here? How weak has Azazel gotten by being stuck here? Azazel reaches for a rock, trying to grab it. I walk over and kick it away from him. Yeah, not gonna happen.

A gray creature with glowing green eyes jumps down from the top of the cave and lands right in front of me. I form a fireball in my hand and throw it at it. The creature catches fire and another one comes. Forming a new fire ball, I aim high over my head. And they run. I turn my cheek to catch Ambrose, useless scythe ready, and Azazel in the form of a very big goat.

"Are you done now?"

Azazel shifts back to his form and Ambrose stretches his

neck, stepping away from Azazel with a disgruntled look on his face.

"That was for casting me away from her as a human, for killing me, and for using Addison."

Azazel nods. "I get it. I deserved all that. Still can't let you win though."

An awkward silence drifts among us.

"Why have you come?" he finally says.

"We should go where we won't be hunted," I say, pointing to the inside of the cave. I don't wait for them to start walking.

"You left me here to die. Why are you back?" Azazel's voice booms through the thick silence, now more serious than before.

Turning my back against the wall of the cave, I reach for Ambrose, wanting him close. Azazel's eyes go from me to him, and he grimaces.

"We're breaking you out," I say.

He pauses, eyeing me suspiciously. "Why?"

Ambrose curls his lips. "Trust me, I'm not fond of the idea."

Azazel scoffs. "Things must be really bad in LLAPS if you want to break me out."

"They are," I say. "And on Earth."

"Why should I care?"

"As if you have another choice, demon. Would you rather stay here forever?"

Azazel scoffs but then silences, peering into me.

"Your father is expecting me to bring you back."

He raises his eyes. "My father is back in LLAPS? You managed to get him to help you?"

The last time I was here, I managed to open a portal to HAPS, in hopes of convincing Lucifer to fix everything. That didn't exactly go as planned. "No, not exactly. But he's in LLAPS now and we all need your help." Azazel puckers his lips and crosses his arms.

"Tell me. Does Lorcan still have my dagger?"

Ambrose flicks his gaze to me. "When did you tell him this?"

"When we were stuck here together."

Ambrose clenches his fist. "I didn't realize you two were on speaking terms back then."

"Aw. Don't worry, nothing happened," Azazel taunts. Ambrose steps forward in his direction. I stop him with my hand.

"Focus." This is going to be a shit show. Ambrose pauses, sighs, and turns around with his hand over his head. "Listen, Lorcan is out of control. He's somehow growing more powerful by eating human souls and the dagger is fuelling him."

Azazel's eyes raise. "Impressive. My work, I mean."

"Well, he's unstoppable now and is controlling all the demons. He even has reapers on his side."

"That sounds like a 'you two' problem."

"Yeah? You don't care that your father is infiltrating the angels who are about to destroy everything—"

"Wait, HAPS is there now?"

"Oh yeah, and dragons too . . ." Not that it makes a difference, but I, for one, still can't get over that.

Azazel's mouth hangs open and then snaps shut. I quirk a brow as he stammers, raises a brow, and looks down. Umm . . . maybe that did make a difference? "I don't know if you realize this, but . . . it's a recipe for disaster. A disaster that could possibly kill me . . . and your kid. And if not us, your baby's home."

Azazel clears his throat and straightens himself up. "Fine. I'll go."

"Like you'd give up the opportunity to get out of here." Ambrose spits.

"Ambrose," I whisper. "Not helping."

"Whatever. Open a portal, *Your Majesty*," Azazel chides.

"I have a few conditions though."

He raises a brow. "Making demands now? I thought you needed my help."

"I do, but you want to get out of here just as bad."

"Go on then, what are your terms?"

"You cannot try to steal the dagger for your gain. You will help take it back and put things the way they ought to be. The moment you try and betray me, *again*"—he flinches—"Ambrose will use that pretty scythe you created to kill you. At the very least, send you straight back here."

He raises his chin and eyes the scythe in Ambrose's hand. "What else?"

I bite my upper lip and hold my stomach. "After this is all over, you will leave me, the baby, and Ambrose alone."

His face slackens and his eyes drop. "No . . . You have to let me see my child."

"Let me remind you, demon," Ambrose starts, "that the relations you forced upon Addison were unwanted and heinous. You will play no part in this child's life." He moves forward and plants two fingers on Azazel's chest, pushing him until Azazel is forced to take a step back. "Or your child will learn the scum its father was."

Azazel's brows narrow. He grabs Ambrose's fingers tightly and curls his lips. Oh, for fuck's sake. I'm about to intervene when Azazel's face slackens, and he releases his grip.

"Fine. Whatever. Let's just go."

No matter how much of a hard ass Azazel is or whatever impression he wants to make on the world, a father will always be undone by a threat toward their child. No father, no matter how horrible, wants their kid to think of them as scum. Pained eyes turn to me.

"Are we going?" he presses.

I nod. "Yeah," I whisper, holding out my hand. A black portal opens inside the cave. If not for its black swirls, I wouldn't be able to see it. The sounds of vents spinning gives me the feeling of urgency. What are we walking into when we cross? Lucifer and Dax went to Earth. The reapers will be rested by now and ready to fight. Or are they fighting already?

Ambrose puts his hand on my shoulder. "Are you ready?" he asks.

"To Earth?"

He nods. Behind him, Azazel looks back to the gray world.

"Would you rather stay?" I ask. "Want to tell your buddies goodbye?"

He turns back to me, his eyes dark and scowling. He nudges his chin forward. I didn't think so. I walk into the portal, Ambrose slightly behind me. Azazel follows and the portal closes.

As we step through, the sun already sets in Tavernier. We're back where we started. Screams of people erupt in my eardrums as we land on the street.

"The demons are spreading farther into the civilians," I say.

Azazel takes a few steps forward and breathes deeply. His eyes turn jet black as he turns to us and spreads his wings.

WAR

ADDISON

"**R**emember our agreement."

"Of course."

"Azazel, I'm serious. Don't do anything stupid."

"Wouldn't dream of it. I hope you're ready for war."

I suck in a breath and look to Ambrose and nod. "I'm ready."

The sound of hooves trotting comes into earshot, a gust of wind stirring with it. A man wearing a red cloak on a red steed smiles in our direction. Or is he only smiling at Azazel? Azazel smirks, spreads his wings, and takes off toward him.

Wind from his wings smacks me in the face. What the hell?

"Azazel!" I yell. I look at Ambrose. "Who the hell is that? He's leaving?"

"Leave him, we need to find the others and formulate a plan. We need a briefing."

"What about Azazel?

"I have a feeling he won't go back on his word. There's too much at stake for him." I shudder a breath.

"Okay, you're right." Ambrose is already checking his scythe for a location. He opens a portal and before I can ask where we're going, he steps through, pulling me along. We step into the midst of tons of people—no, zombies—walking, reaching out aimlessly. Some drooling from their faces, others bloody. An acrid stench fills my nostrils and I move my hand to my face.

"More zombies?" Great, no progress was made while we were away.

"Over there!" Ambrose points in between the mob of undead walking. A growl I recognize comes between them. That's definitely Skadi. My brother and Evander follow behind her.

"Dax! Over here!" I run over, pushing zombies off me, almost forgetting I can use my powers to throw them off. My hand glows hot as I throw a surge of light in between the mob, creating a clearing.

"That's handy," Dax says. "We were avoiding using deadly force in case we can . . ."

"Somehow find a cure? Yeah, me too, but I'm not sure that will be possible. They seem lifeless in there . . . just a walking, hungry corpse."

"Where's Lucifer?" Ambrose asks. Good question.

"He took off shortly after we got here. Said he had a friend to wake up."

"War," Evander chimes in.

I squint at him. "Excuse me?"

"He meant he was waking up War."

My mouth drops. "War . . . as in from the four horsemen? *That* War?" Gooseflesh prickles my arms. The man on the red steed. Holy shit.

"That'll be the one, hence all the undead."

"I don't understand . . . Isn't that a bad thing? Wouldn't that bring on the actual apocalypse?"

"Well, so far he hasn't called down Pestilence or Famine so . . . I think he was hoping War would help defeat HAPS. He mentioned something about finishing what they started a long time ago." I gulp. More zombies push themselves through the street. This is insane.

"I guess that makes sense, though, if Azazel was the first angel of death," Dax says.

"Right. I forgot about that."

Dax grabs onto Skadi's neck to hold her down. "We've been trying to save as many souls as possible. Skadi is getting better at following directions. But the bad news is . . ."

"There's more bad news? The literal four horsemen isn't enough?"

"The hypnotic spell has spread farther. I haven't found a demon who isn't under Lorcan's command."

"And the angels?" Ambrose asks.

"Since War has gotten here, they've dispersed. Probably strategizing."

"And the reapers?" I ask.

"They're out helping us do the same thing we were doing. Reaping, basically."

"Smart move," Ambrose adds.

"What about Azazel?" Evander asks.

"He left the moment we landed. No matter. I think the plan now is to locate Lorcan and put an end to this. Any news on his whereabouts?"

"According to the Akashic, he's still hiding in his pocket dimension."

"We need to bait him out."

I dart a look at Ambrose. "How?"

A vent opens behind me. "We can help with that." I spin around to face Azazel standing next to a giant man atop a big, red steed. Holy shit, that guy's big. "Lorcan is after you because our child threatens him."

My eyes grow big.

Ambrose lays his arm out in front of me, pushing me back. "Absolutely not."

"No harm will come to her," Azazel says.

"I don't trust you."

Dax arches his brow. "What the hell are you implying?"

Oh shit. He means to use me as bait. "I'll do it," I say abruptly. He's right.

"Hell no, Addie. Are you nuts?" Dax raises his voice. "He almost killed you last time! The man is unstoppable."

"Over my dead body," Ambrose says.

"It's my choice. Azazel is right. He can hide out forever and wait for the perfect opportunity to strike."

"I don't like this," Ambrose says. I turn to face him, putting my hands on his shoulders. His eyes try to move away from me, but I make him look at me, moving my gaze to his.

"It'll be okay."

"You can die."

"I won't die. I have you to protect me. And Azazel won't let anything happen to his baby."

"You have my word as well," War says. "This is the best strategy."

"I refuse to believe that," Dax says.

"I'll be guarding you as well, in dragon form," Evander chimes in.

"See? I'll be safe. Besides, I'm not completely powerless, you know."

Ambrose sighs. "There's no talking you out of this, is there?"

"Nope."

He tightens his jaw. "Fine," he mutters under his breath. "But you will listen to my command, Addison, and . . ."—he grunts—"Azazel's and War's. Don't go off on your own, do you hear me?"

I chuckle. "Mhmm . . ." As much as I do not like being bossed around, it is kind of hot coming from Ambrose. And I do understand why he's doing it.

"I'm serious, Addison. Tell me you understand."

I smile and show my teeth.

"And if it gets too dangerous, get out of there!"

"We'll play that by ear."

"Addison!"

I lean in and kiss him. That shuts him up. He stumbles back a bit, but I keep hold of him, sliding my tongue in his mouth; my leg pops up as I lick the inside of his teeth. He slows down and grabs my back, kissing me passionately. I know everyone is watching us, but I don't care. Azazel clears his throat. I grin into Ambrose's face and pull away, leaving him blushing.

Ambrose sighs. "Please be careful."

Azazel coughs and I spin around to see his disgusted, pissed-off face.

"Okay, I'm ready. Let's do this."

Ambrose checks his scythe, turning the dial, just as portals open and reapers zip down from the air.

"They're moving in!" Evander yells. Ambrose grabs my hand and uses his scythe as a shield against them as they spread out amongst the zombies.

"There's no time." Azazel grabs my arms and pulls me away from Ambrose's grip. Ambrose breaks neck and reaches for me, but I shake my head. "I love you," I mouth to him, then turn and run with Azazel through the undead mob.

"Where are we going?"

"Trust me."

"Yeah right, fat chance!"

He races toward a gray parking garage and bolts for the stairs. "It's better if we're away from all the zombies and at a higher vantage point." Oh. Fine. I bolt through the doors after him and run up an obscene amount of stairs until we make it to the top. Gasping for breath, I pass through the door as he holds it open for me.

"Now you're a gentleman?"

"You're welcome," he sneers. "And I've never not been a gentleman with you."

"Uh . . . I beg to differ."

He rolls his eyes. "I apologized. I told you, the way I was brought up . . ." He sighs. "I realize my methods aren't always right."

I glance at him. "Is this a real apology?" Oh my god. But still. I can never forgive him. This is probably just another manipulation anyway.

He looks up and sighs. "Just stand somewhere in the center."

I look over to the empty rooftop. "What are you going to do?"

"Lurk in the shadows till he shows up. When he does, I'll surprise him."

I give him an unsettling stare. Am I really trusting Azazel right now?

"Don't worry, I'll be close."

I swallow and slowly make my way over to the center. After minutes of waiting, I start to look around. Where'd

Azazel go to hide exactly? What if Lorcan has been listening in from behind the veil and is onto us. I could be standing here all day while I could be out rescuing prisoners. I should have brought Skadi with me. She'd at least be here keeping me company.

More minutes pass and I start to grow antsy. Azazel, still nowhere to be seen. What if he got distracted and left somewhere? He does seem flaky like that. Or . . . I gulp. What if he has some other motive? No . . . he cares about his child . . .

A portal opens and a reaper steps out. I brace myself. Shit, here goes. Expecting it to be Lorcan, I create a fireball in my hand. I might not have dragon fire, but I can still use it to defend myself. A regular skeletal figure with a normal blue scythe comes out. Umm . . . Not Lorcan. Another comes out and then another.

I back up, more reapers emerging from the portal. Shit. I'm outnumbered. I look from side to side, to see if Azazel is anywhere. No such luck. What is he doing?

I freeze the rooftop below us, causing thick ice to form. One reaper slides as it walks, but it doesn't seem to bother them much. Vines emerge from the back of the building, sliding around me and wrapping themselves around the reapers. Their scythes glow, burning my vines straight off. "Okay shit bags, for my next trick"—a surge of wind comes from my palms—"I'll blow you right off the building." I'm running out of ideas here. Reapers are dead. How am I meant to kill them? I wish Evander had come with us instead, but I know he's looking for his cousin.

Wind snaps one of the reaper's heads off and it shatters to the ground. I wince. The others don't seem to notice or care and keep coming at me. I hit them with another gust of air.

The reaper's faces frown at me as they force me back until I'm hitting the ledge with my foot. Now would be a great time for this asshole to turn up.

A portal opens up high above us. I crane my neck and gasp as Lorcan flies down from it, his body glowing with a strange gold light, surely from the souls he's been gorging on. This asshole will do.

The reapers make way as Lorcan floats down, positioning himself in front of me, his hair billowing behind him. His eyes are completely white, like his hair, and he holds my dagger in his right hand. His pale face, humanoid, is soft though, with a square jaw. Something's different. He's been altered somehow. Could he be even more powerful?

My eyes fall to the glowing ruby hilt of my dagger.

"Right now, as we stand, War is down there creating more zombies. You foolish girl, you've fallen right into my trap."

My lips part. No, that can't be . . . I look around for Azazel. Nowhere to be found. He'll come. He cares about the life of his unborn baby. He will come.

"A demon like Azazel won't care about you or his demon spawn. He knows he can just make another." My cheeks burn and my stomach starts to twist.

"You're wrong," I choke.

"He used you to get out of his prison. That's all. And now, he'd feed you to me while he and his daddy use War to take over."

My mouth gapes, and I search for him desperately. Lorcan strides closer and I kick a rock from under my foot down the building. Could he be right? Of course. How could I be so stupid? We never should have trusted him. My hands heat up, fire burning bright in my palms, and I turn them toward Lorcan. I'm not going down without a fight. Lorcan guffaws, and I throw a fireball straight to his face. It hits him and diminishes to ashes the moment it makes contact. I throw another and he keeps moving toward me. My power does nothing to him now. He raises my dagger, now inches away from me, and lunges it to my chest.

A bright red glow blinds me and it takes me a moment to realize the glow is coming from the scythes of the reapers around us. Lorcan arches a brow and looks behind him. The reaper's eyes are now glowing red. One of them stabs Lorcan from behind and he drops to the floor, my dagger dropping to the ground with a clank.

I suck in a breath as I reach for it, but Azazel pops in front of me and grabs it before I can. He did come back.

"W–what are you doing?" I stammer.

"Taking back what's mine." He turns to Lorcan, the dagger glowing bright in his hand. The reapers have all stopped looking at me and Azazel, and are fixed on Lorcan, their eyes still burning red, as well as their scythes. Shit . . . Azazel is controlling them now! He advances toward Lorcan, who has righted himself. However hurt he was a second ago didn't last. As much as I want Azazel to kill Lorcan, I don't like that he's taken control of the reapers . . .

"Azazel . . . remember our agreement." Don't do anything stupid.

Azazel grunts. "That place made me weak. I needed more power."

"Azazel, for the sake of your child."

He snaps his attention to me. "You won't win against me, Addison. Back off."

Lorcan laughs. "Take the dagger. I no longer need it, it's yours."

My eyes widen and I stare at him. It's true then . . . His power has surpassed the dagger's.

"We'll see about that." Power radiates from the dagger's hilt to the tip of the blade just as the reapers move toward Lorcan, seizing him tightly. Electricity hits Lorcan's chest from the dagger, and for a minute Lorcan seizes. The power stops, the dagger still glowing in Azazel's hand. My eyes switch back to Lorcan, who . . . Ah, shit.

He snickers and breaks loose from the reapers' grips. I stumble to the side, too close to the cliff of the roof. Azazel advances, swings his arm, and punches Lorcan straight in the jaw. Lorcan backhands Azazel across the face, making him hit his face on the cement of the ledge.

I should probably help him back up . . . but . . . Yeah, nah.

Lorcan spreads his arms, and just as he's about to do something, my wings shield me. Between my feathers, a sweep of light shines through. When I lower them, Lorcan is nowhere in sight.

"What the hell happened?"

"The reapers . . . He killed them."

I spin around, my spine tingling with fear. He killed . . . all of them at the same time? "How?"

Azazel gets up and leans his rear against the ledge. "He's right. He's harnessed enough human souls to no longer need the dagger's power."

I take a moment to let that sit. Sounds of the battle continuing below us echo in my ears. Before I can say anything else, Azazel gets up and starts walking.

"Woah, where are you going?"

"To kill Lorcan. And then take down the angels."

"Umm . . . we both just witnessed Lorcan killing off all those reapers at the same time, and you just said it yourself, he doesn't even need the dagger anymore. So how exactly are you going to kill him?"

"Oh, I won't be doing it by myself."

"Then how?"

He holds up the dagger. "By taking back control of every demon and reaper here. He can't win against all of them."

"No, wait . . . Azazel . . . What do you mean by control? Why not just take command of them?"

"Because I'm including the angels as well. And the way I'm about to do this, I can't have one without the other."

I screw up my face. *What?*

"Oh, and that'll include your mother and boyfriend."

"We had an agreement!" I run up and spin him around. "Don't do this!"

"I have to. This is how I get things back to the way they were. He might no longer need the dagger, but he's still connected to it, which means it can still kill him. Just needs more manpower."

"But not this way . . . Azazel, please. Don't take them away from me . . ." I run after him, grabbing his arm. He spins around and steps forward forcefully, pushing me back.

"That golden scythe *is mine!* And with this, I can get it back!"

"Azazel . . . We had an agreement. You will not see your child."

He guffaws. "As if you can keep it away from me."

Rage burns my face and I start hitting him. One punch after another uncontrollable punch. He swings his hand and hits me across my chest, lunging me away. My wings catch me as I hit the ground, breaking my fall. My heart beats fast as I get to my knees. He's gone. *Fuck!*

MORE POWERFUL THAN THE DEVIL

ADDISON

I quickly open a portal and run out to the zombie-infested street. I gasp as all around me are red scythes, glowing bright against the dark of night. Oh shit, oh shit, oh shit. I push the walking corpses away, desperately looking for my brother, or Ambrose, anyone I recognize. Up ahead, I hear the clashing of metal. A battle is still breaking out. The angels. I pick up my pace and start pushing my way through the zombies. A bark comes from ahead. Skadi? I make a beeline toward the barking and as soon as I see her, she runs full force at me. I wrap my arms around her big neck. "Skadi, where's Ambrose?"

She pulls away and starts running, so I follow. Hoping to the gods she's leading me to him.

BOOM!

My heart stops. Skadi skids on the ground, pauses, and keeps running. Without taking a moment to catch my breath or unblur my vision, I dart out after her. That had been the sound of the angels throwing a bomb. Besides the countless reasons why they could—zombies, demons, rehypnotized reapers under Azazel's command, Lorcan,

War—all I want is for Ambrose and my brother to be safe.

BOOM! BOOM!

I'm thrown against a car, my wings guarding me from danger. Droplets of fire rain down on me as I struggle to get up. Pieces of debris are everywhere. I wait to hear from Skadi . . . a yelp, a growl, a bark, something! But her barking doesn't come. Tears well up in my eyes.

Please don't let that bomb have hit . . . I swallow. *Please don't her be dead.* Fire blazes around me as I stumble. Looking for survivors, I spot a demon lying on its side, headless, blood gushing from its neck. Beside it, a head . . . Tentacles where a jaw should be.

Oh no, Cthulhu-guy. I start toward it but stop when I hear a growl. Skadi? I turn and see my hellhound sniffing around a statue of some type . . . A statue of an angel. It takes me a moment to realize I've walked to a cemetery. Behind it is the silhouette of two figures. My heart beats in my throat and I make a run toward it.

"Just think of it as a self-sacrifice." Azazel's voice comes from behind the statue. I move in a little closer.

"The scythe will never let you touch it." Ambrose's voice hits me like a pile of bricks. I'm not too late. I stop running and hide behind a nearby tree. Off to the side, Lucifer stands with my brother. They're unmoving. Why aren't they doing anything? Lucifer has a stupid smile pasted on his face while my brother frowns, his dark eyes not moving from Ambrose.

Beneath me, the ground quakes. What's going on now? Rotten arms pull themselves up from the gravel. I grab onto the tree, keeping my balance. Groans come from the tombs as the dead rise.

"Unlike the zombies Lorcan created, these will help

defeat HAPS." The dagger glows in Azazel's hand at the same time, as do the empty corpses. They start walking toward the street.

"They won't get started until I get there, and this part I am finally going to enjoy." He takes the dagger and points it at Ambrose, the tip of the blade touching his neck. I stifle a gasp. He must be under some immobilizing spell. That's what it is. Azazel has Ambrose under his immobilization spell. The same one used on Dax when I was cursed and thought Dax was my boss. Back when I thought Ozo was calling the shots, but it had been Azazel all along, pulling the strings. Dax is probably afraid if he tries something, it'll get Ambrose killed faster. I need to break that spell before Azazel kills him.

My eyes fall on the golden scythe, sticking up from the ground.

I dash for it, jumping over tombstones and a short bush. I keep running. I have no idea what it'll do to me, but I can't just stand around waiting to see what happens. Azazel's eyes sparkle. I think I hear my brother screaming at me from the distance, and somewhere between that is Lucifer's maniacal laugh.

I probably shouldn't touch the thing that chooses its owner. The weapon created by Azazel himself to kill all immortals. But I'm not an immortal. At least not yet. Not fully.

I curl my fingers around it and wince, expecting it to blast me to oblivion, or back to purgatory. But . . . it doesn't. I let out a sharp breath. A smile curls on my face. I pull it up from the ground and point it to Ambrose. Like all magick I've practiced, I envision him being released from his invisible shackles.

It works. Ambrose topples forward from being held in

one place, his face pale—well, paler than usual—as he stares at me holding the scythe in disbelief.

Hoping it reads me the same way, I turn the heavy blade to face Azazel. I take one heavy step forward, carrying the scythe with both arms now, forcing him to step back.

"You know what this can do," I spit. "Seeing as how you made it."

"Put that thing down, woman!" Lucifer screams, but I ignore him. Right now, I'm pretty sure I'm more powerful than the devil.

Azazel grows pale in the face. "Addie . . ."

"I told you not to fuck with my family. I guess this is where I kill you." I take another forceful step closer to him and he trips over a tombstone and falls to the ground. I point the tip of the curved blade to him, and a sweep of purple light shimmers over the blade. This power is far more than anything I've ever experienced. I can almost feel a distant connection to the Akashic, but it's a feeling I know doesn't belong to me. I put it aside for now and focus on Azazel's frightened stare.

"Addison . . . I—"

My frown deepens. I can touch and hold the scythe. I can take the dagger from him too. "We don't need you." His fingers coil around the dagger, drawing it up.

"Don't make me defend myself against you, Addison." Realization strikes me. We might kill each other in this process.

"Give me the dagger," I say.

"No."

"Give it to me, or I will kill you."

"You still can't defeat Lorcan without me. I couldn't by myself, and you don't have what it takes to do it."

"Yes, I do."

He laughs and inches himself up off the tombstone. "No, no you don't. But I do."

"I've had enough of your attempts to control me and everything and everyone I love. Goodbye, Azazel." I tip the scythe down, and just as a stream of power bleeds from the tip, it floats above him. What the hell? I try again, and this time the power ricochets off him and hits a nearby tree. A tiny rumble hits my stomach just as my braided hair lifts from my shoulder. I gasp and Azazel laughs. The baby. I lower the weapon.

"Addie?" Ambrose's voice interrupts as he steps forward, taking the scythe from me.

Azazel laughs harder, a tear in his eye. He wipes it away and lies back against the stone. "Oh . . . I don't think our baby wants you to kill me."

My face pales. "No . . . no, it doesn't." I stumble back and my brother comes to steady my footing.

Azazel wipes himself clean and flicks his gaze to Ambrose. "Fine then, you get to live, reaper. But as War kills, more undead are being created."

Around us, reapers and demons with red eyes, being led by War, fight angels. Another bomb goes off in the distance.

"I'll still annihilate the angels and reapers. Lorcan will be the last to go. Then my father and I will take HAPS."

"Take HAPS? There'll be nothing left for you to take," I say.

"There's always more."

Another bomb hits, and this time I look. Lorcan is floating high above the ground, electricity leaving his fingers and hitting the dead beneath us, shooting everything down, demon, reaper, and angel alike.

Someone runs toward us from the fire.

"Ambrose! Dax!" Evander sprints toward us and my

brother weaves to him. Ambrose squeezes my arm, pulling me with him. I start to move but glance one last time at Azazel.

His grin and the twinkle in his eyes die as he looks past me. My brows furrow and I crane my neck. A dragon chases Evander through the buildings and heads straight for us.

"Blaise is back!" Evander screams.

RING OF DRAGON FIRE

ADDISON

zazel takes an unsteady step forward. Despite Blaise's rain of fire soaring overhead, there's something in Azazel's features that I can't shake.

"Addison, we have to move!" Ambrose's voice brings me back to the present.

"Son!" Lucifer runs up and pushes Azazel out of the way. Azazel doesn't budge though. He stumbles a little, but his face grows solemn as he stares at Blaise.

Blaise lands behind me, heat surfacing heavy on my arms. Ambrose's hoarse scream shatters my ears as my heart drops to my stomach. I spin around and no longer see him. Did he get flung somewhere?

A circle of dragon fire gets cast around me and I sweat. The flames rise high to where I can no longer see over them. I'm trapped.

Blaise faces me head on as she lands on her own fire, her whited out eyes staring at me. Does she even feel her own burn? If she ever does come back, that's going to hurt. "Hey girl, long time no speak. You okay?" Sweat beads down my forehead.

She roars, fire burning from her nostrils. My wings enclose me, but now the fire is too hot, too close. I summon water like I did before. It trickles down, but . . . this time it's different. The more Blaise breathes fire, my water boils. Did Lorcan do something to empower her? Or is there just too much flame?

She blows fire again and I hit the ground. Through my wings, I try to peer between the flames. *Dragon fire can kill reapers.* Shit . . . Where did she throw Ambrose?

"Blaise . . . Come on, I know you're still in there . . ." Her white eyes glaze over me. She can't hear me at all.

Fire soars overhead again. I duck, my wings protecting me. This time, my feathers singe and a cry escapes my throat. Come on, water! Power surges through my arms, water comes from the ground but boils again. I hop on it. Okay, bad idea. There aren't any walls I can make the water come down from. And as much as I'd love to make it rain, I cannot control the weather. I'm powerful but not that powerful.

"Blaise! You're going to kill me!" I shout despite knowing I can't get through to her. Fire breathes out of her nose again and I turn around, letting my wings encase me once again. They burn like hell. That's one appendage I never thought I'd get to feel pain in. Damnit, Blaise!

She can finish me off if she wants to. Why is she trapping me here, taunting me?

My knees wobbly, I stand. My cheeks burn from the fumes of the fire surrounding me. Hopelessness chokes at my throat. I'm at a loss for how to get out of this. Blaise's iridescent horns reflect off her fire as she sends me another blow.

I fall to the ground, dizzy as everything grows hazy around me. I try to summon water one more time, but my energy is so low I don't think I have enough juice even if I could.

Someone jumps through the flames. I can hardly see them, but they lift me up, pulling me up by my arms.

"Addison." That voice . . .

"Azazel?" I mutter weakly.

"Addison . . . You were right."

"What?"

"I know what I have to do."

"*What?*"

My vision comes back and I see him. Azazel jumped through dragon fire to get to me.

"I have to destroy the dagger."

I shake my head slowly . . . "No . . . why . . ."

"No time to explain. I tried to use it on the shifter to break the spell, but it didn't work. Lorcan is nullifying all magick. Pretty soon, not even I will be able to stop him."

Throat dry, I rasp, "H–how do you destroy it?"

"Leave it to me, I created it. There's only one way to destroy it, and that's by using my power *and* dragon fire. And I won't survive the blast. So, it's now or never." Wait, what?

Blaise roars furiously, fire hitting the both of us. Both my and Azazel's wings cover us. Bringing us closer. From inside our cocooned wings, Azazel grabs my face.

"What do you mean you won't survive the blast?" I say.

"Never mind that. There's no time. You have to promise me something first."

I stammer, "What?"

"Do not give up your immortality. For the sake of our child."

"But . . . I'm not . . ."

"No. I said listen. You will be. And you will watch empires rise and fall while you live forever. Take our son or daughter, fix their broken wings . . ." He sucks in a breath, as if trying to keep his voice from cracking. "You have to be there to teach them to fly again when they fall."

"What the hell? Azazel . . ."

"And one last thing . . . Once I do this, Lorcan will be less powerful. You'll be able to kill him with the scythe. Killing him at this point is the only thing that will keep our child safe. I'm making sure it has a home and a living mother. And that, Addison . . . It truly is important to me." His voice rises.

"Okay . . . but I still don't understand. What do you have to do?"

"Addison, you have to make me that promise . . . Seeing this dragon . . . it reminded me . . . of someone I loved who wouldn't want me to be this thing I am now."

"I can't—"

"Addison, I beg of you. Our child will need you. Don't let them grow up the way I did."

I swallow.

"Will you promise me?"

I nod. "Y–yes . . ."

The heat intensifies. Azazel grabs me and pushes me out of the flame. I land hard against Ambrose.

"Ambrose! You're okay!"

"Yeah, a little hurt but alive—"

"Run!" Azazel's voice booms.

Ambrose and I get to our feet and sprint away from Blaise. I grab my brother's arm on the way and Evander also runs with us. I turn for a second just as a wave of bright orange fire erupts from the circle.

Lucifer runs toward the fire screaming, "Noooooo!"

My eyes widen as a bright light sweeps the ground, blinding me. As it settles, I realize I'm gripping Ambrose's arm hard and loosen my grip. A giant circle of ash surrounds the area, but no dragon. I take a few steps forward and see Blaise in human form standing at the center of it. Her knees quiver and she falls to the ground. Evander runs to her.

I gasp when I see Lucifer drop to his knees. He picks up Azazel's body. And he weeps. The image of the devil crying over his dead son sends a chilling wave of despair I did not know I could feel.

"Is he . . ." I approach him, cautiously. My breath hitches and my voice quivers as I see him. Azazel is dead. And the dagger is gone.

Ambrose puts a hand on my shoulder. "Addie . . ."

I clutch my chest. I should be happy . . . but I'm not.

"There's still a war happening around us," Ambrose urges.

"And speaking of War . . ." my brother says just as War approaches on his giant steed, closing in behind Lucifer.

"He was a good man, Lucifer. Let me take him back."

Lucifer stands and nods. "We still need to finish this."

I bite my lower lip. Our relationship wasn't the best. It's probably wise I make myself scarce.

"The bombing has stopped for now," War declares. "The angels have noted a shift happening." War turns to me. "What did happen?"

"He–he said the only way to save his child is to kill Lorcan, and the only way to do that—"

"Was to destroy the dagger. Because it's what kept Lorcan strong," Lucifer finishes.

A tear strolls down my face. The sound of Azazel's voice before he died . . . He really did care.

Blaise clears her throat. "If it's alright with you, I'm about to go roast myself a reaper."

OPERATION UNHYPNOTIZE

ADDISON

The angels are gathered at the center of Mallory Square when we arrive. The rising sun makes my eyes hurt. Dry and scratchy after hours of being awake, not to mention the interdimensional jet lag—and being pregnant. After all this, I'm sleeping for a week!

Over by a gazebo, I can see my mother tending to some of the injured. The dead around us have fallen. No more zombies. I guess the dagger's magick had more control over Lorcan's power than the magick he developed.

"This doesn't mean he's undefeated though," Ambrose says, reading my mind.

I look at him, still unable to find my words.

Some demons crawl over from the road with white eyes. "We still need to unhypnotize them."

Ambrose turns a dial on his scythe and holds out his hand. "Why don't we do that?" Just as I'm about to grip his hand, a gust of wind pushes me forward as Lorcan floats out from a portal behind us.

Ambrose and I exchange a glance, and he raises his scythe to Lorcan. "We'll have to do it later," he shouts. "Time to lock up a rogue reaper." I stifle a bemused scoff at that last thing. Without the dagger . . . can we stop him? Is what Azazel said before he died true?

Evander and Blaise, already shifting to dragon form, advance from behind us. Lorcan's eyes are still a bright white as he lowers himself to the ground, silver electrical light swirling around his hands. His face twists in unwavering hate as he points his fingers upward. A blast of electrical heat lands on dozens of angels and demons. Ambrose slams his scythe on the ground, and with a purple sweep, the electricity ricochets out toward the street. The ground shakes under me but I ready myself to help him take on Lorcan.

Reapers, no longer under Azazel's control, come out, with their scythes pointed at him, ready to strike him down. Electricity shoots out from Lorcan's hands again, but one of Ambrose's reapers blasts a shield of ice to stop it. Yes! Ten points for our team!

Blaise leaps over my head and into the sky as fire soars from her nose, singing Lorcan's hair. He falters, his eyes now going from white to normal . . . Evander shoots fire at him again just as Lorcan creates a barrier to block it from hitting him. Now, Blaise swoops in closer, her mouth wide open. I gasp and cover my mouth just as she picks her legs up, reduces speed, and chomps down on his torso. Blaise rips him to shreds. Evander takes his other side, and they split him apart. I watch in horror as they let him drop, and then catch the rest of his bits on fire.

"Holy . . . shit . . ." Dax mutters. My voice is still caught in my throat.

Back at the Reaper Council training room, reapers tend to the injured. What's left of Lorcan's reapers have been put in a holding facility to deal with later. Dax stayed back with Evander as he collected lost souls from Lorcan's damage, while Evander "cleaned up" using the forgetful-device-thingy. Blaise also went with them, but my suspicion is that she went to tag along with Dax.

I plop myself down on the lounge area couch while Lucifer and my mother argue to high heaven about the history of HAPS, grudges, being a control freak, and I don't know what else. Skadi jumps up and rests her head on my lap. I scratch her behind the ears while I listen. My father comes to sit on the opposite couch from me, Crowley keeping his distance, weary of Skadi's presence.

"You listened to—no, manipulated—a dead man to take control—"

"I didn't manipulate anybody, I wasn't even around back then—"

"Listen to yourself, you *are* HAPS! If you continue acting in the old ways, then take responsibility for the past, or change!"

I sit back and listen. No need for me to get involved in *that* argument. Although, watching my mother argue with the literal devil is kind of funny. Considering no one, not even my father, ever wanted to argue with her when she was alive. I exchange a glance with my father.

"What do you think is going to happen?" I ask.

"Well, I don't know. But whatever does, I have a feeling the afterlife is going to be different."

"Hmm . . ."

My father lifts his arm for Crowley to land on it, patting the bird on the chest. For a second my mind drifts and I tune out the noise. *The longer you're a demon, you'll become immortal.* I place my hand on my tummy and start rubbing it unconsciously as my mother still argues.

"Dad?" I pull out the small bottle with the purple and gold potion in it. "Back at HAPS, my mother gave me a potion." His face stiffens. "This will allow me to become human, stripping me of all my demon powers."

He stares at me, and I swallow. I'm not sure I want that for myself anymore, but . . . do I really want my child to live a life being a demon?

"What about the baby?" my father asks.

"It will turn the baby human as well . . ."

He sighs. "If that happens, Addison, there's a caveat you should consider."

"What?"

"When stripping you of your demon powers, it will wipe out any demon blood in you, the type of blood that allowed you to enter the astral dimension as a mortal. You may be able to still practice magick, but you'll have to retrain yourself from the beginning."

My lips part . . . I had forgotten about that. My baby will be human and will be able to live a human life . . . But I'll never be able to return here. Ambrose and my brother will visit, so that won't be a problem. But my baby won't ever know this place. Not sure that's a bad thing though. Azazel's words echo through my head . . . *Promise me.* I shake it away.

"Just thought you should know."

I twist my features and stick it back in my pocket.

"And what do you expect to do? You have a terrible reputation. It's even reached Earth, Lucifer."

"And you lot have destroyed the planes." He crosses his arms.

I clear my throat and they both stare at me. "I just

wanted to say that he was saving demons while on Earth . . . from Lorcan's command."

"Yes, *mija*, but those are demons."

I stand. "Well, maybe he's right then. If you're going to put value on the higher astral, over the lower astral, then you're not fit to lead, Mother. Keeping everyone segregated is backwards. You should know, that happened on Earth. It seems the system in the astral is no better than up there. Maybe Lucifer's methods were foul back then, but I believe, as I've witnessed, he does have our best interests at heart. He's still an angel who believes in choices, not command with no questions asked."

Lucifer crosses his arms and smirks. My mother grabs her head.

"It's not that I believe in command with no questions asked . . . That's just how it's always been done."

"Well, I think it's time for a change."

Ambrose walks between the reapers, who are now looking better and dispersing. "Those who are ready, get to reaping. There's work to do." He smiles at me and comes over.

"There you are," I say.

"Did I hear you agreeing with Lucifer?"

I chuckle. "Maybe . . . But I'm starting to see what he means. After getting to know the angels, he's right. There needs to be a change and, despite Lucifer's methods, he has everyone's best interest at heart. I can't argue with the need to question things."

"You're right." He smiles again and kisses me on the forehead. He turns to my mom. "Would it be so hard to work with Lucifer up in the higher levels? He does have experience and there are higher-level demons up there, like Paimon and the horsemen, who will follow his lead."

My mother puckers her lips. "Alright."

Lucifer's mouth drops.

"On one condition."

Lucifer sighs and stares at her through lowered eyes.

"You'll be overthrown the moment you scheme for your personal gain."

"I never intended to do that anyway. I only wanted others to question authority. The unanimous efforts of HAPS are what creates 'God,' and without questioning, you get a dictatorship. That was never what I wanted."

My mother nods. "Well, this might be difficult to break to the angels, but I'll try."

"I'll help," Ambrose adds. "And Evander is on his way to negotiate with the Sidhe commanders about sharing the waters."

I place a hand on his shoulder. "I think a unanimous effort between the planes is probably best."

"So, *Judge,* I take it you'll be in charge of the reapers?" Lucifer asks.

"I don't plan on giving up being the Judge anytime soon," Ambrose says with a smile.

For someone who didn't want it, he's come a long way. "It suits you," I say, giving him a kiss on the cheek.

"So, who will watch over the demons?" Lucifer asks, glancing at me. "You're still not wanting to take up the mantle?"

My face reddens and I glance down. "Honestly? I don't think this place is fit for a baby. No offense, but Azazel had a hard childhood."

Lucifer grows silent.

"And it'll be long before the planes are fully in agreeance."

"If ever," my mother adds.

"Right . . . And I think . . ." I swallow. I'm breaking Azazel's promise, but . . . he left me no choice to object when he asked. "It's best if my kid is human and goes to school . . . and lives a normal life."

Lucifer nods. "Well, I won't force a decision on you."

"If I take the potion"—my mother gives me an appreciative look—"then I can never return here in my human form, so neither can your grandchild. I'm sorry."

His face pales.

"But," Ambrose begins, "*we* can still visit *them.*"

Lucifer nods. "And you're sure you want to take the potion?"

"I am."

"Then I'll see you at the child's birth."

I offer him a smile and turn to my mom. I give her a tight squeeze. "Some epic fight, huh?"

"Yes, at least it's over."

"Well, there are still things to discuss. Like, now that the old Judge isn't around to make reapers out of souls, and keep humans in their own prisons, what now?"

I turn to Ambrose. "Yeah, Judge, what now?"

"I was going to ask you what you suggest, actually."

"Me?"

"Yes."

I twist my face. "Well, humans die and come down, to live either in eternal torment, or go to HAPS, right?"

"Well, yes, but no one has come to HAPS in hundreds of years," my mother says.

Oh right, I remember Azazel saying that. "What if we allow humans to have just enough awareness. To learn through their torment—on their own, or perhaps with a little help if needed—and when they are ready, allow them the choice of returning to Earth to try again, or going to HAPS. Or becoming a reaper."

Ambrose chafes his chin. "So, they would choose to become reapers if they want?"

"Better yet," I say, "what if they learn and are integrated back into society—by means of reincarnation. They could become reapers, be mentored."

"That's one way they can learn the value of life," Ambrose weighs in.

I nod. "That way, they don't end up in eternal torture nor go back to doing the exact same thing they went to hell for."

"Those born of demon blood can stay if they want. But demons will be given new roles," I add.

"Such as what?"

"Anything they want. Just like Earth. I'm sure there's plenty that needs to be done around here."

Lucifer smiles plainly. "I like that. We'll take it under advisement under the new rule."

"Yes, we'll take it under advisement in HAPS," my mother corrects. "New rule." She rolls her eyes and chuckles. I give my mom another hug and my father stands up and does the same.

"Bye mom, I love you."

"I love you too, *mija*."

"Will I get to see you again?"

"Probably not for a long time."

I swallow a tear and hold her tighter. Angels from HAPS don't visit Earth. The only ones who do are reapers. "At least come with Lucifer on special occasions?"

"Okay, I can do that, I guess, under the *new rule*." She smiles.

I turn to Ambrose and grab his hand, leaving my father behind to talk to my mom so that we can have a moment. "I guess . . . I'll be seeing you and my brother on Earth from time to time?"

"Sooner than you think."

"But . . . how often?"

"As often as before, wasn't that good? I won't leave you to raise the baby on your own, Addie. I made you a promise and I intend to keep it."

"I know . . ." I guess it'll be like military families, except in our case it'll be everlasting. He draws me in and plants a kiss on my lips. I take in the softness of his lips and let all my worries wash away.

"You can't get rid of me that easily," he says.

"I love you."

He kisses me again.

My father approaches a few steps behind, and I turn. "I guess we should get home. We have a lot of cleaning and groceries to do," I chuckle.

"And I have to implement that protection on Earth so that this doesn't happen again."

We step over to the side, and I glance back one last time. At the reapers, and at Skadi, who sees me looking at her and comes running. I bend over and grab her monstrous neck. "You can't come with me this time, Skadi. Be good to Ambrose and Dax, they'll take care of you."

"Oh, we have a better use for these hounds now," Ambrose says. "Going to put her to work, help collect souls. Don't worry, they won't eat any this time."

I chuckle. "Hear that, Skadi? You're getting a job." She yelps and licks my hand. I stand up and turn toward an open space.

"I'll be back with Dax for a proper goodbye," he says.

"You better." I slant my smile and then open a portal to Paradise House.

EVERY ROSE HAS ITS THORN

ADDISON

My father and I step into the cold air conditioning.

"Ah, perfect, the air is working again!" I say.

"Was it broken?"

"Oh, you have no idea what went on in this house while you were away. Luckily, Ambrose fixed it all with his scythe."

The house feels weird now without Skadi running around and making a ruckus. And Dax getting angry at her. I make my way down to the bar, something I had been avoiding since I expect all my plants to be dead.

I pick up one of my rosemary pots. Some of its dead leaves crumple on the floor.

Yep. All dead. I sigh. Well, I'll just have to start over and plant new ones. Setting the pot back down on the windowsill, a sense of loss washes over me. I'm going to have to call work. What do I even tell them? Surely, they would have noticed my absence even with Evander's fix. Last time I entered Seashore Memorial, my coworkers ended up dead. Now that Florida has gone back to normal—or what's normal for Florida— I wonder what the police would make out of what happened.

Do I even *want* to go back to nursing? It seems like a lifetime ago.

I go back upstairs to take a shower, get ready to clean and do groceries. It feels odd having to get this gunk off me before getting dirty again cleaning, but I have blood on me and went through an epic battle. Not to mention, I'm starving and need a nap. My stomach roars and I rub it, looking down.

"But yes, food first."

A week passes and I still haven't seen Ambrose or Dax. So much for coming back soon to give me a proper goodbye. I sit at the breakfast table in the kitchen, clutching the small bottle in my hand, twirling it around and watching the gold swirl through the purple liquid.

"Are you going to take it?" My father interrupts my thoughts as he comes in and opens the fridge. Crowley perches by the window and starts tapping to get in. I unlatch the door and push it open just enough for him to fly inside.

"I wanted to, but . . ."

"Then don't, Addie."

"What?"

"You know, I never tell you what to do. You've always had a good head on your shoulders, and I've always let you make your own decision. But in this case, I really don't think you should take it."

"But—"

"Addison, if you're feeling like you don't know how to go back to the way things were, it's because you never can. You, as much as you don't want to admit it, will never be the same again."

"I know, but—" I place my hand on my stomach.

"Do you really want to lie to your child, and take away their true nature? Has this whole experience taught you nothing?"

Promise me you'll never give up your immortality.

I swallow my guilt. "On the one hand, Azazel told me not to let his child grow up the way he did, and on the other, he ordered me not to give up immortality. That feels like a catch 22. I don't know what to do."

"Your child will never grow up the way he did, because it has you as its mother."

I nod, a faint smile spreads on my lips.

"*Mija*, listen to me." He takes a seat. "You made a difference in the lives of countless demons who felt unwanted and unloved, with no direction. Born to be bad. And they wanted to follow you. You have the chance at immortality." He places his hand on mine. "*Take it.*"

"But what about you?"

"What about me? I'm an old sorcerer with demon blood, I can take care of myself. Besides, that enchantment I created?"

"You mean the sigil? What about it?"

"It protects the planes, but, I haven't enacted it yet."

My brows raise. "What? Why not?"

"Because it does something else too . . . but I was waiting for you."

"I don't understand."

"If you stayed human, I couldn't do it. But if you decided to go back, I would put it over the house as a pocket dimension. So that you could still live here, but here would be in the same timeframe and plane as LLAPS. The neighbors would still see the house, and could still see us whenever we're inside."

I gasp. "You didn't . . . ! And it'll work?" This is way different than the warding I put in place earlier. Mine only protected the house. Not to mention, it didn't stay in the same timeframe as LLAPS.

He scoffs. "Of course it'll work, who do you think I am? Curses, Addie, don't insult me."

I laugh and hug my father.

Someone clears their throat at the entrance of the kitchen.

"Dax!" I get up and run to him and Blaise walks out from behind him. "And Blaise!" I throw my arms around them both. "But where's Ambrose?"

"Right here."

A giddy smile pastes on my face and then I force it away. "Took you long enough! Seriously, after the last time you didn't show up!"

"I know I know, I'm sorry . . . we had a lot of cleaning up to do . . ." I throw my arms around him and kiss him.

"It's okay." I let go of him but place my hand on his cheek and he leans into it. "I have some news . . ." I choke.

"Is that coffee I smell?" Dax interrupts. "You have to try some Cuban coffee," Dax says, already heading for a cup in the cabinet.

"Okay, coffee first, then news."

"Oh?" Ambrose crinkles his nose as if it's already brewing.

We sit around the breakfast table, sipping our coffee and laughing. Blaise has three cups—I don't want to be anywhere near her in dragon form after that much coffee. After drinking the last sip, I set it down and tell everyone to follow me outside. We stand at the dock, the hot sun radiating down on us.

"You couldn't tell us whatever it is inside?" Dax pulls on his collar.

I laugh. "Patience. My father right now is inside enacting a spell to bring the house into LLAPS' dimension."

Ambrose screws up his face. "Wait—but then—"

"Hold up," Dax starts. "If you do that, how are you going to be in the astral as a mortal?"

I take out the bottle from my pocket and hold it up.

"Oh, she hasn't taken it yet," Blaise says smugly. "Well, well, well, one of us, one of us."

I give her a funny look.

"Your brother has been making me watch movies," she says.

"Wait, I'm confused," Ambrose says. "Addie, what are you talking about?"

I clear my throat and walk to the edge of the dock. "I have decided not to take the potion." I pull open the cork and chuck it in the water. His mouth drops, then his eyes gleam as he looks at me.

"Wow," he says.

"Yes, wow."

"So, what now?"

"Well, I guess um . . . Show me to my throne?"

Dax cracks up.

ONE YEAR LATER

"Oh my god, Addie, he's adorable!"

"Thanks, Ava," I say, taking baby Deacon-Marcello back from her.

"Thank you so much for doing this for Padrino."

"Don't mention it. I wanted to have done something sooner, but ruling demons proved to take up all of my time. Oh, and whenever you want to visit the house, just let me know and I'll have my dad lift the dimensional shield. My cell phone works as long as I'm at the house." I wink.

"That's so cool. I still can't believe you're a demon queen," she says.

"She's *the* demon queen." Ambrose comes in and kisses me on the forehead. "How's little Deacon doing?

"He's fussy, can you take him?"

"Of course." Deacon coos as Ambrose lifts him from my arms. Outside, thunder roars. What the hell? I go to the window and roll my eyes. That's no thunder. That's Dax coming out of his portal with his altered motorcycle.

"Seriously, Ambrose . . . Did you really have to go and fulfil my brother's Ghost Rider fantasies?"

"I wouldn't be a good friend if I hadn't. What? It suits him." Blaise jumps off the back and I crack a smile. A dragon who can fly, clutching to my brother on his bike. I can't make this stuff up.

My mother and Lucifer pop into the living room shortly after, next to Madrina, who yelps at the sudden surprise of a portal opening next to the chimney.

The door slams shut and Dax yells from the first floor. "Got the Key limes! Who wants Key lime pie martinis?"

Ava's eyes widen and she makes a dash for the stairs. I laugh and the rest of us follow her down.

"How soon do you have to go back?" Ava asks as we get to the first floor.

"Oh, not too soon. I left some trusted reapers in charge of the demons while I'm gone. And with the hellhounds helping the reapers, things go a lot smoother."

"Looks like you guys have it all figured out."

"Well, mostly. Now, figuring out how to raise a demon baby with archangel blood? That's going to be a whole new challenge on its own."

Get the prequel free when you sign up for my mailing list at
http://killianwolf.com/

As a reaper my life is simple . . .

Go where I'm told, help the dead move on. No bonding. No
interfering with mortal affairs.

Collect, guide, rinse, repeat.

But when an escaped demon starts killing off a little boy's family
one by one and affecting the balance of the universe, am I
expected to stand by and watch?

Or should I save him, even at the expense of my existence?

ACKNOWLEDGEMENTS

I have to say, Addison fought me over this book being the last one in the series. She even offered a spin-off idea for a new series at the end.

Thank you so much for reading these books! This was my first urban fantasy series and while I had to unpublish and rewrite the first three books, I had a blast living in LLAPS and hanging out with both reaper and demon-kind.

A huge thanks to my editor Claerie Kavanaugh. My voice and skills has become stronger because of you.

To my husband Michael. See? Told ya I'd finish writing this series! Not that you ever doubted me. Now we can toast and celebrate from Bristol to Key West. Especially because now, I really want some Key Lime pie.

And to you, my readers! I can't say this enough— thank you so much for sticking with me and reading until the end. Without you, this would not have been possible.

Come say hi in my Reapers and Demons Facebook Reader group. In there, every day is Halloween!

facebook.com/groups/killianwolf

Keep updated about my next series and new releases when you join my mailing list, if you haven't already.

killianwolf.com

facebook.com/killianwolf22

twitter.com/killian_wolf22

instagram.com/killian_wolf

amazon.com/Killian-Wolf/e/B07WHFB8FW

bookbub.com/authors/killian-wolf

goodreads.com/killianwolf

pinterest.com/killianwolf22

ABOUT THE AUTHOR

 Killian Wolf is a Miami, Florida, native who enjoys pirates, rum, and skulls as much as she loves writing about dark magick and sorcerers. She holds a Bachelor of Arts degree in Cultural Anthropology and Sociology and a Master of Science in Environmental Archaeology and Palaeoeconomy.

Killian writes books about obtaining magickal powers and stepping into other dimensions. She lives in England with her husband, a tornado of a cat, and the most timid snake you'd ever meet. When she isn't writing, you might find her at an archaeological dig, rock climbing, or sipping on dark spiced rum while working on a painting.

www.ingramcontent.com/pod-product-compliance
Lightning Source LLC
Chambersburg PA
CBHW021134190726
48288CB00008B/2651